쓰이거나 쯔이거나

아시아에서는 《바이링궐 에디션 한국 대표 소설》을 기획하여 한국의 우수한 문학을 주제별로 엄선해 국내외 독자들에게 소개합니다. 이 기획은 국내외 우수한 번역가들이 참여하여 원작의 품격을 최대한 살렸습니다. 문학을 통해 아시아의 정체성과 가치를 살피는 데 주력해 온 아시아는 한국인의 삶을 넓고 깊게 이해하는 데 이 기획이 기여하기를 기대합니다.

Asia Publishers presents some of the very best modern Korean literature to readers worldwide through its new Korean literature series 〈Bilingual Edition Modern Korean Literature〉. We are proud and happy to offer it in the most authoritative translation by renowned translators of Korean literature. We hope that this series helps to build solid bridges between citizens of the world and Koreans through a rich in-depth understanding of Korea.

바이링궐 에디션 한국 대표 소설 065

Bi-lingual Edition Modern Korean Literature 065

# Puy, Thuy, Whatever

# 백가흠
## 쁘이거나 쯔이거나

# Paik Ga-huim

ASIA
PUBLISHERS

Contents

# 쁘이거나 쯔이거나

## Puy, Thuy, Whatever

노모가 맨발로 마을 어귀까지 아들을 마중 나왔다. 쉰
이 넘은 아들을 부여잡고 뺨을 어루만졌다. 노모는 시
종 씨의 뒤에 어쩔 줄 모르고 서 있던 쯔이를 보더니 인
상을 찌푸렸다.

야여? ……야가, 아직 앤개벼.

짐을 받아 들며 노모는 큰아들이 데리고 온 여자를
아래위로 훑어봤다. 그러곤 고개를 숙이고 서 있는 쯔
이를 눈으로 채근했다.

엄니한티 인사드래야지.

쯔이가 눈을 마주치지 못하고 까딱 고개를 숙였다.

The aged mother came out bare foot to meet her son there, at the entrance to the village. She threw her arms about the son, over fifty himself, and she rubbed his cheeks with her hands. Then the aged mother looked over and grimaced at the sight of Thuy, just standing there behind Shi-jong and not knowing what to do.

"That her? ...Nuthin' but a baby, yet!"

Taking the bundles from her son, she looked her over, up and down, the girl her older son had brought back. Her eyes bore into Thuy, who stood there, hanging her head.

"Well, ain't you gon' greet yer mother?"

9

이름이 뭐이?

이름이 쁘이여.

쁘이? 우리말은 전혀 못 하능 갑네. ⋯⋯피부가 너매 까맨 게 아녀? 니 말론 한국 사람 같다도만, 통 아니고 만. ⋯⋯아를 나면 튀기 표가 팍 나겄시. ⋯⋯이렇게 쪼맨헌 야가 밭일이라도 할 수 있겄냐?

시종 씨는 헛기침을 하더니 둘의 시선을 피하곤 앞서 걸어갔다.

오매, 너 우냐? 왜 우냐잉?

눈물이 터진 건 시종 씨가 성큼성큼 멀어져간 순간이었다. 돌아서 가는 그의 등을 보자 서러움이 한꺼번에 몰려나왔다. 믿고 싶었던 무엇이 막 허물어졌다. 가까스로 붙잡고 있던 가느다란 줄이 툭, 하고 끊어졌다. 막막함이 자꾸 눈앞을 어지럽게 만들었다. 그녀는 쭈그려 앉아 서럽게 울기 시작했다. 집 앞까지 갔던 시종 씨가 뛰어 내려왔다.

엄니, 왜 아를 울리고 그려요.

얼레, 내가 멈시롱 했다 그러냐. 그냥 주저앉아 울고만. 아직 시엄니한티 인사도 없음시, 애 나라 예법이 이

Thuy couldn't meet her eyes, but she dipped her head, once.

"Whut's 'er name?"

"Name's Puy."

"Poo-wie? Guess she don't speak the language none? ...Skin's sure dark, ain't it? Don't look a bit Korean, not like y'said... Ever has any baby, baby's gon' look a mix... Think she c'n work the field, runt like her?"

Shi-jong cleared his throat, and he turned away from their looks and walked on, ahead of them.

"What's this? Cryin'? W'you cryin' for?"

It was at the moment when Shi-jong had gone on, moving on his long strides away from her, that her tears had burst forth. All at once, when she saw him turn his back and break away, sorrow had swelled and rushed over her. This was the crashing collapse of what she had been determined to believe in. That fine thread on which she had just managed to maintain her grip had suddenly snapped. Her sense of helplessness sent everything before her eyes spinning, again and again. She sank into a crouch and wept in anguish. Shi-jong had almost reached the house, and now he was running back.

렇다냥? ……기가 맥히구마잉.

시간이 흘러도 쯔이가 그날 처음 느꼈던 막막함은 사라지지 않았다. 가족들의 사랑이 유일한 위안이 될 수 있었겠지만, 그러기엔 아직 서로에게 시간이 부족했다.

쯔이의 유일한 위안거리는 가족들이 아니라 바로 TV를 보는 것이었다. 쯔이는 한국에 온 뒤로 온종일 TV 앞에 앉아 있었다. TV를 보는 동안은 외롭고 서러운 생각이 들지 않았다. 음악 방송과 재방송되는 드라마 안에 그녀의 많은 오빠들이 있었다. 그녀의 코리안드림은 가요와 드라마에서 시작했다고 해도 과언이 아니었다. 쯔이에게 그들은 천상에 사는, 이상과 꿈속에 사는 사람들이었다. 고로 그들의 나라, 한국은 쯔이에게 이상과 꿈이었다.

이 사람들이 가수란 말여? 당최 이런 걸 몰라서……

쯔이가 수첩에 가지고 다니던 동방신기의 사진을 내밀었다. 시종 씨는 양손으로 양쪽 옆머리를 긁적였다. 벗어진 정수리를 가린 부분 가발이 답답해서 죽을 지경이었다. 가려운 곳은 못 긁고 옆머리를 연신 긁어댔다.

한국 가면, 동방신기, 볼 수 있어?

"Wha'd you make her cry for, Momma?"

"What? I 'nt say nuthin Just sits down and starts cryin.' Never even gave her mother-in-law no greeting. That their custom in her country? ...Damned if I know what."

Time passed, and yet Thuy was not able to get over the sense of helplessness she had known for the first time that day. Only a family's love could have consoled her, and they had shared yet too little time.

But then Thuy's only consolation never did come from the family, but from watching television. That was how she spent her days after coming to Korea, sitting in front of the TV. She didn't feel her loneliness at those times, while she was watching TV, and she wasn't sad. There were her guys, so many of them there in those concerts and those re-runs of old serial melodrama. It would not be wrong to say that her dream of Korea had begun with Korean pop songs and this Korean serial melodrama. For Thuy, these were the people who dwelled in paradise, who lived in the ideal and in dreams. Thus Korea, their country, had been her ideal and her dream.

"Them's singers? Well, I wouldn't know 'bout any

동방신기? 그럼, 만날, 테레비 나와. 서울에 방송국도 많아. 한국에 가자마자, 쫘악 서울 귀갱부터 하잖게.

쯔이는 시종 씨에게 처음으로 웃어주었다. 시종 씨는 뭐가 뭔지도 모르면서 그녀가 자신을 보고 웃어주는 것이 좋아서 따라 웃었다. 그는 확신할 수 있었다. 이번에는 장가갈 수 있겠다고.

우리, 서울, 가요?

별 볼 것도 읎어. 사람만 많고, 정신없고. ……엄니가 눈 빠지게 기다림시룽, 얼렁, 가자고잉.

쯔이는 비행기에서 내리자마자 남편과 함께 공항버스를 탔다.

……네에.

별일 아니었지만 그녀는 불안해졌다. 사소한 약속을 지키지 않는 것이 더욱 그러했다.

앞으로 살아야 할 집으로 가는 길이 아주 멀게 느껴졌다. 이상하게도 베트남에서 한국까지의 거리보다도 공항에서 집을 찾아가던 그 길이 더욱 먼 것 같았다. 공항에서 탔던 버스는 전주에서 섰고, 다시 버스를 갈아타고 구불구불한 산길을 두 시간 가까이 달렸다. 쯔이

a' that..."

Thuy was showing him the photos of Dong Bang Shin Ki that she carried in her pocket book. Shijong scratched with both of his hands at the sides of his head. The hair piece that covered the top of his head made him very uncomfortable. And because he couldn't scratch the spot that itched, he just went on scratching away at the sides of his head.

"If I go to Korea, can I see Dong Bang Shin Ki?"

"Oh yeah, Dong Bang Shin Ki? Sure, they's on every day, on the TV. Seoul got all these broadcasting companies, you know. Soon's we get to Korea, first thing, gon' hit Seoul, take in every bit of it."

For the first time, Thuy smiled at Shi-jong. Shijong didn't know what to make of any of this, but pleased by the way she was looking at him and smiling, he smiled back at her. Yes, he was sure of it. He was going to get himself married, this time.

"Are we...going...to Seoul?"

"Aw, ain't nothin' to see, there. Too many people, that's all, an' y'can't even think... Listen, Momma'll be anxious, lookin' for us to get in, so maybe we'll just get going."

Once off the plane, Thuy and her husband were

는 남편과 함께 외진 마을, 동안리라는 곳에 내렸다. 덕유산 자락, 시종 씨의 고향마을이었다. 그곳은 인천공항에서도 너무 멀었고, 서울에서도, 하물며 가까운 대도시인 전주에서도 먼 곳이었다. 쯔이는 난감한 마음이 들었다. 그때서야 자신이 꿈꾸었던 코리안드림은 화려한 도시, 대도시 안에 있다는 것을 알았다.

어떠? 산 좋고, 물 좋고. 내가 농사지으며 평생 산 곳이여. 이제 알콩달콩 쯔이랑 함께 살 곳이고.

쯔이는 시종 씨의 말에 아무 대답도 하지 않았다. 시종 씨는 버스에서 내려 성큼성큼 걸어갔다. 동네 입구에서부터 신이 나서 고함치며 자기 어머니와 동생을 불렀다.

엄니, 엄니! 색시 왔슈. 기종아, 기종아! 얼렁 와서 형수님한테 인사드래라.

쯔이는 시어머니와 시동생과 함께 사는 줄은 몰랐었다. 인천으로 오는 비행기 안에서 그의 가족에 대해 처음 들었다. 생각해보니 남편에 대해서 아는 것이 거의 없었다. 남편도 마찬가지였겠지만. 쯔이는 현실에 직면하고서야, 뭔가 잘못됐다는 것을 뼈저리게 느꼈다.

16

on this bus from the airport.

"...Okay."

In itself, it was not important, but she was growing uneasy. What was worse was his failure to keep his promise, even if it had been over a trivial matter.

It seemed to her a long way, the trip to the house where she would from then on have to live. Strange, but the distance from the airport to the house seemed to be even greater than the distance between Vietnam and Korea. The bus they had boarded at the airport stopped in Jeon-ju, where they transferred to another bus, and from there they continued on roads that went winding through the mountains for almost two more hours. Thuy got off with her husband at a remote village called Deung-an Li. This was Shi-jong's home-town, at the foot of the Deok-yu Mountains. The place was far from Incheon Airport, far from Seoul and far from even Jeon-ju, the city nearby. This would be a struggle, for Thuy. It occurred to her then that what she had dreamed of Korea must be in the cities, so grand and so splendid.

"Well, whutch'er think? Got some beautiful mountains, got clear water. 'S'where I been farmin',

쯔이는 버스에서 내린 자리에서 쉽사리 발을 떼지 못했다. 금방 울음이 빵, 하고 터져 나올 것만 같았다. 꼭 다문 입술이 부들부들 떨렸다. 당장 뒤돌아 도망치고 싶고, 이제 먼 나라가 되어버린 자기 고향으로 돌아가고 싶었다. 가족을 떠나 낯선 이국에 펼쳐진 운명을 받아들이기에 그녀는 너무 어렸다. 자기가 왜 이곳에 있어야 하는지, 자신의 어리석음이 무엇이었는지 판단하기에 쯔이는 아직 어린 나이였다. 저 멀리서 맨발로 달려오는 그의 어머니가 보였다.

시종 씨는 한국으로 시집온 뒤로 매일같이 울고만 있는 어린 신부를 다독이느라 애를 먹었다.

쪼매만 지나면 괜찮아질 거랑게롬.

쯔이도 그의 말을 믿고 싶었지만 그는 자신에게 아무것도 줄 수 없다는 것을 알았다. 그녀가 원하는 것에 남편은 없었기 때문이다.

시어머니의 유별난 아들 사랑도 남편과 가까워지는 것을 막는 이유 중 하나였다. 쉰이 넘은 노총각 아들이었지만, 시어머니에게는 아직 어린애 같은, 금쪽같은 큰아들이었다. 남편은 그녀와 관계 맺지 않는 날이면

m'whole life. An' now it's where me an' Puy's gon' live, all nice and happy."

Thuy did not respond to what he had said. Once off the bus, he was on long strides, and at the entrance to the village, he called out to his mother and his brother, excited and shouting.

"Momma! Momma! M'wife's here! Ghi-jong! Ghi-jong! Come on now, and say hello to yer sister-in-law!"

Thuy had not known that he was living with his mother and his brother. It was only on the plane, on their way to Incheon, that she had heard for the first time anything about his family at all. When she thought about it, she found that she knew almost nothing about him. It was the same for her husband but, facing this fact, she was hit hard by a sense of something wrong.

It was not easy for Thuy to proceed from where she had gotten off the bus. She seemed to be on the verge of sobbing, in tears. There was a hard tremble in her lips, which she held pressed tight. She wanted to turn and run away and to go back to her country, which had become such a very distant land. She was too young and could not accept it, that her destiny would unfold here, in this foreign

노모와 함께 잤다.

　시종 씨도 점점 지쳐 쯔이에게 시큰둥해졌는데, 예외
로 잠자리에서는 열정적이었다. 쯔이는 남편과 관계 맺
을 때를 빼고는 언제나 혼자였다. 남편이 그녀를 찾는
횟수는 점점 늘어났지만, 마음은 더욱 멀어져만 갔다.
남편은 이제는 아예 서둘러 일을 치르고, 노모의 방으
로 건너갔다. 쯔이는 벌거벗은 채 남편이 사라진 문을
멍하니 바라보았다. 힘들었지만 매일 밤마다 치근덕대
는 늙은 남편, 시종 씨를 거부할 수가 없었다.

　남편, 오늘은 쉬어요. 저, 몸 아파요.

　얼레, 만날 집이 있는 애가, 니가 뭘 했다고 아프냐잉.
내가 금방 끝낼 팅게. 쪼매만 참어.

　왕성한 남편의 성욕 때문에 그녀의 몸은 편치 않았다.
쯔이는 저녁을 먹은 후에 밖으로 나가 오래도록 서성였
다. 남편을 피할 수 없다는 것을 알고 있었지만, 마음이
답답하고 방 안에 가만히 있을 수가 없었다. 축사에 쭈
그리고 앉아 그가 잠들기를 기도했다. 거실로 나와 함
께 TV를 보거나 가족과 함께하는 것을 시어머니가 싫
어해서 거실로 나올 수도 없었다. 시어머니가 집에 있

land that was so strange to her, with her family left behind. So young, she could not see any reason that would explain why she had to be here, but neither could she understand how foolish she had been. Some way off, she could see his mother, running and bare foot.

Shi-jong tried to comfort his young bride, who had done nothing but cry, every single day since coming to Korea to enter the house-hold of a husband, but it was hard for him.

"You hang in there, just a little more, I promise it's gon' get better."

Thuy wished she could believe what he said, but she knew there was nothing he could give her. A husband was not among the things she desired.

Another factor that kept her from getting close to her husband was the mother-in-law's extreme love for her son. He was over fifty and an old man, but to her mother-in-law, he was the precious son, and still a child. Her husband slept with his aged mother, whenever there were no conjugal relations.

Shi-jong grew tired of Thuy and came to have little interest in her, though he still had exceptional desire in bed. Thuy was always alone now, except

을 때엔 그녀는 방에서 나오지 않았다.

시종 씨가 나름 성교에 집착하는 데에는 이유가 있었다. 쯔이에게 들인 돈 때문이었다. 그냥 잠자리에 들면 마음이 뒤숭숭해졌다. 쯔이를 그냥 내버려두는 것이 왠지 뭔가를 손해 보는 느낌이 들었다. 들인 돈이 아까운 것은 아니었지만, 쯔이를 가만히 놔두는 것도 찜찜했다. 장가 못 간 동생을 생각하면 더욱 그랬다.

소개비로 선금 8백만 원을 내고, 원정 선을 보러 나갈 때마다 3백만 원씩을 더 내야 하는 고비용 결혼 프로젝트를 통해 쯔이를 만났다. 그는 벌써 베트남에만 두 번째였고, 중국과 우즈베키스탄에도 한 번씩 다녀왔다. 그녀를 만나기 전, 이미 선금 포함해서 2천만 원가량이 들어갔다. 들어간 돈 때문에라도 결혼이 더욱 절실했다. 결혼을 하게 되면 신부 집에 지참금으로 5백만 원을 더 지불해야 했으니, 이만저만 돈이 들어가는 것이 아니었다. 촌에서 기를 쓰고 농사를 지어보아도 1년 남짓 걸려야 버는 돈이었다. 자기 먼저 얼른 장가를 가고, 뒤이어 동생, 마흔여덟 살 먹은 기종 씨도 장가보내줄 참이었는데, 계획대로 되지 않아서 시종 씨는 동생 기종

when there were conjugal relations with her husband. Her husband was requiring her with more
frequency, and yet her husband's heart went farther and farther away. Now, her husband would
finish quickly, and then go off to the aged mother's
room. Thuy, naked there, would just gaze over at
the door through which her husband had disappeared. It was hard for her, but she could not re-
fuse Shi-jong, the old husband who bothered her
every night.

"Husband...maybe today a break? My body... It's
not well."

"What? At home every day, how could you be
wore out? Hang on now, I'll be quick."

Because of her husband's vigorous sexual desire,
her physical condition was not good. After dinner,
Thuy would go and wander about for some time.
She knew she couldn't avoid her husband, but she
felt an anxiety, and it was not possible for her to
stay in the bedroom, calm. So it was out in the
shed that she would sit, praying for her husband to
fall asleep. The living room was not an option, as
her mother-in-law did not approve of her there in
the living room, watching TV with the family. When
there was just her mother-in-law at home, she

씨를 볼 면목이 없었다. 불만 없이 사정을 기다려주는 동생에게 그는 더욱 미안했다. 돈 때문에 동생 기종 씨는 해를 넘겨야만 했다. 예상했던 것보다 돈이 두 배로 들어갔기 때문이다.

성이, 꼭 장가보내줄게. 쪼매만 참아라잉. 니 형수처럼 젊고 이쁜 여자로잉. ……내가 가본께 너는 활달해서 우주베키스탄 애들하고도 잘 어울릴 것 같어. 그쪽도 아주, 갠찮애. 늘씬하고 아주 갠찮애.

동생 기종 씨는 뒷머리를 긁적이며 쑥스러워했다. 시종 씨는 베트남에서 돌아온 후, 돈을 너무 많이 들인 것이 미안해서 동생을 볼 때마다 하루에도 몇 번씩이나 같은 말을 반복했다. 그는 동생 장가보내줄 몫까지 돈을 써버렸다는 사실에 마음이 착잡하기만 했다. 화장실에 가는 기종 씨를 붙잡고, 젖소에게 여물을 주고 있는 기종 씨를 붙잡고, 세끼 밥상에 마주 앉을 때마다 같은 말로 미안함을 표현했다.

아이고, 성, 난 갠찮애. 천천히 햐. 성 장가간 지 얼매나 됐다고 그려. 사정이 그리 있는 것도 아니고. ……찬찬히.

would not come out of her room.

There were reasons for Shi-jong's fixation on sex. There was the money that had been spent on Thuy. If he went to bed without sex, he felt troubled. He felt that by leaving Thuy alone, he was somehow taking a loss. Although he did not regret the money that had been spent on her, leaving her alone didn't seem right to him. He felt this way even more when he thought about his younger brother, who still wasn't married.

The expensive marital program through which he had met Thuy had first required that he pay eight million *won* for the broker's services, and then there had been an additional three million *won* for each of the acquaintance trips. He had already made two of these trips to Vietnam, and he had been once to China and once to Uzbekistan. Even before meeting her, he had gone through something like twenty million *won*, with the cost of the broker's services. Having already spent that much money, he was desperate to get married. And then in the event of marriage, five million won had to be given to the family, so it was an enormous sum of money that had gone into this marriage. Out in the country-side, it would take more than a year to

아녀, 내가 니 몫까지 써갔고, 마음이 그래 그려. 동상, 내년 봄인 무신 일이 있어도, 젖소를 다 팔아서라도 장개보낼 팅게.

참으로 우애 좋은 형제였다. 동생 기종 씨가 고등학교를 다니느라 전주에서 보낸 3년을 빼고는 둘은 50 평생같이 붙어 있었다. 형은 동생을 최고로 똑똑하고 진득한 사람으로, 동생은 형을 가장 부지런하고 능력 있는 사람으로 알고 살았다. 그렇게 붙어 있었어도 살면서 서로 큰소리 한번 오고 간 적이 없이 우애가 돈독했다. 흔히 남자 형제들이 자라면서 벌이는 우격다짐도 그들에겐 없었다.

……정, 못 참겠음시 니 성수 함 빌려주고.

동생 기종 씨의 눈이 휘둥그레졌다. 젖소에게 착유기를 달고 있던 기종 씨가 뻔히 형을 쳐다보았다. 착유기가 젖꼭지를 벗어나며 엉뚱한 곳에 붙었다.

성님, ……그시, 무신……

엉뚱한 곳에 착유기가 물린 젖소가 움머, 하고 울었다.

에고, 이놈아 농담이여. 허허허허. 너, 깨딱허단 소까

26

make that much money, even if he threw himself into the farming.

He had intended to have his forty-eight year-old younger brother, Ghi-jong, get married, once he had first gotten married, himself, but his plan had not worked out, and now it was difficult for him to look at the younger brother, Ghi-jong. So he felt especially bad about it all, as his younger brother went on waiting, without complaint. The younger brother, Ghi-jong, would have to wait for one more year for the money. He had spent twice as much money as he had expected.

"Older brother's gon' get you married, guaranteed. You hang on, jus' a little more. Gon' be married, and she'll be young and pretty, jus' like your sister-in-law... Tellin' you, speakin' from experience, out-going guy like you, get on fine with one a' them Uzbek girls, even. Very nice. Slender an' all that, real nice."

This would cause his brother, Ghi-jong, to scratch the back of his head, embarrassed. After coming back from Vietnam, Shi-jong was so sorry about having spent so much money that he would say the same things over and over. He was in conflict over it all, because of the fact that he had

정 잡겄다. 언릉 바로 혀. 소 젖퉁이 아프다잖여.

기종 씨가 고개를 돌려 착유기를 제대로 소에게 달아주자 소가 울음을 멈추었다. 아무리 농담이라지만 기종 씨는 당황한 마음을 감출 수가 없었다. 모든 것이 다 까발려지고 들켜버린 것이 아닌지 조바심이 일었다. 화들짝 놀란 것이 티 나지 않았을까, 그는 슬금슬금 형의 눈치를 보았다. 혹시라도 형이 모든 것을 눈치채고 자기를 채근하는 것은 아닌지 두려웠다.

성님도, 참. ……그런 농담 마랑게. 안 그려도, 여자 하나 없시 속이 시커먼디. 그리 놀리고……

너, 내가 농담했다고 성났냐?

기종 씨가 토라진 듯 축사를 나갔다.

야, 야. 미안타. 정말, 장난이여. ……성이 잘못혔어.

멀어져가는 기종 씨를 보며 형은 난감한 표정을 지었다. 성큼성큼 막사를 벗어나는 기종 씨의 마음은 도무지 진정이 되지 않았다. 이 일을 어떻게 수습해야 할지 막막했다. 울음이 터져 나오려는 것을 그는 꾹 입술을 깨물며 참았다.

살면서 형제간에 처음으로 생긴 작은 틈이었다. 서로

spent even what was supposed to have been his brother's share of the money. Ghi-jong might be on his way to the bathroom, or might be giving fodder to the milk cows, but he would stop him and express his regret, always with the same words, as he also did at the table, where they sat across from each other for all three meals.

"Okay, okay, big brother, I'm fine. Take your time. You just got married. It ain't necessary... Slow down."

"No, I spent your share a' the money, and I ain't comfortable 'bout that. My little brother. I'm a git you married next spring, no matter what, even if I got t'sell every one a them cows."

They truly were good brothers, getting along well and with affection. Except during the three years his younger brother Ghi-jong was in Jeon-ju to attend high school, the two had dwelled together throughout the fifty years of their lives. To the older one, the younger brother was a smart and patient fellow, while to the younger one, the older brother was a fellow of the greatest diligence and ability, and so they lived, each thinking of the other in this way. Living always together, and each spending that much time with the other, still they

는 그것이 어색해서, 저녁 밥상에 마주 앉았을 때도 다른 날과는 달리 많이 웃지 않았다. 형이 슬쩍 동생의 기분을 떠보았으나, 맘이 풀리지 않았는지, 동생은 그냥 건성으로 형의 농을 받아주기만 했다.

시종 씨는 동생을 무슨 일이 있어도 해를 넘기지 않고, 장가보내야겠다고 다짐했다. 내일이라도 당장 농협에 가서 대출이라도 알아볼 참이었다. 자기 인생 없이 형의 농사일을 뒷바라지하느라 늙어버린 동생이 안쓰러워 마음이 착잡했다. 고개를 숙이고 밥만 먹는 동생이 불쌍해서 형은 괜스레 눈물이 나왔다.

남편은 어린 신부에게 순간마다 모든 게 잘될 거라고 말했다. 이상하게 남편이 하는 그 말을 들을 때면, 쯔이는 모든 것이 엉망이 되어버릴 것만 같았다. 그녀는 지금, 남편과 함께 있는 이 순간이 불행하다고 느꼈다. 이런 감정이 미래에 더 큰 불행을 몰고 올 것만 같았다. 쯔이는 얼마 전, 시종 씨 몰래 읍내에 있는 산부인과에서 낙태를 했는데, 그게 다시 불행의 시작처럼 느껴져서 두려웠다. 한국에 온 지 다섯 달째, 그녀의 눈은 허공만 바라보고 있었다. 쯔이의 시간은 한없이 더디게 흘렀다.

got along so well and never had any serious con-flicts. In brothers, there is usually a tendency to fight, but these two never did.

"...Well, it gets to be too much for you, let you borrow your sister-in-law."

The eyes of the younger brother Ghi-jong went wide. He was just then hooking a milking machine up to a milk cow, but Ghi-jong now stared up at his older brother. The clip missed the teat and got fastened at the wrong spot.

"Older brother... I mean, well, what..."

The machine being fastened in the wrong place, the cow cried out.

"Hey, you dumb-ass, it was a joke. Heh heh, heh! Look out, now, looks like you gon' kill that cow. Hurry up, put it right. Cow says her udder's killin' her."

Ghi-jong brought his head back down and fas-tened the machine at the right spot, and the cow stopped crying. Maybe it had been only a joke, but Ghi-jong could not hide his shock. He was wor-ried, afraid that everything had become apparent or been discovered. His shock being extreme, he wondered if it would not be obvious. He stole glances at his older brother, trying to find out. It

멍하니 앉아 있는 시간이 많아졌다. 쯔이가 해야 할 일은 매일 산더미처럼 쌓여 있었지만, 그녀는 아무것도 하지 않았다. 시어머니의 구박이 느는 것은 당연했다. 모든 것이 싫고 귀찮아졌다. 한국에서의 결혼 생활은 시작도 해보기 전에 벌써 실패한 것 같았다. 무엇보다, 믿고 살아야 하는 나이 많은 남편, 시종 씨가 사랑스럽지 않았다.

남편, 씻고 와. 몸에서, 이상한, 냄새, 나.

아니, 뭔 냄새가 난다고 그려. 방금 씻고 온 사람헌티.

시종 씨는 킁킁거리며 자신의 몸 구석구석 냄새를 맡았다. 쯔이는 남편이 옆에 오면 가급적 숨을 참았다. 그에게서 참을 수 없는 역겨운 냄새가 났다. 실제로 냄새가 나는 것인지 아닌지는 확실하지 않았다. 냄새 때문에 그녀는 점점 남편 옆에 있기가 고통스러웠다. 관계 맺을 때마다 숨을 참느라 그녀는 죽을 지경이었다. 그나마 관계 후에 남편이 노모의 방에서 자는 게 차라리 다행이었다.

뿌이, 사랑혀.

남편이 그렇게 말할 때면 쯔이는 팔에 오소소 소름이

was perhaps just possible that his older brother knew everything, and that this was an interrogation, and he was afraid.

"Yeah, ah, sure, older brother... Don't mess w'me like that. Bad enough, havin' no woman. You never let up."

"You angry, then, 'cause a my joke?"

And so under a disguise of anger, Ghi-jong went out from the shed.

"Well, hey now. I'm sorry. Really. It was a joke... Your older brother made a mistake."

The older brother's face showed his struggle, as he watched Ghi-jong moving off, away from him. And Ghi-jong, stomping away from the shed, could not begin to pacify his own heart. Shi-jong had no idea of how to handle this mess. Pursing his lips tight, he was just able to hold back his own tears.

This was the first time in their lives that even a small rift had come between the two of them. Sitting across from each other at the dinner table, both felt awkward, and they didn't laugh as much they did on other days. As the younger brother made only mechanical responses to his jokes, the older brother, doing what he could to know the mind of the younger, surmised that he must be still

돌았다. 남편은 가끔 그녀에게 연민을 느낄 때면 사랑한다 말했다. 간혹, 나이 어린 신부가 먼 타국에서 자신에게 시집온 것이 안쓰럽고 불쌍하게 느껴질 때가 있었다. 고단하기만 한 농촌에서의 삶 때문에 시종 씨는 더욱 미안한 마음이 들었다. 쯔이는 그런 시종 씨의 마음이 고맙기는커녕 불편하기만 했다. 시종 씨와 관련된 무엇도 도무지 마음에 드는 게 없었다. 처음부터 그랬다.

쯔이는 그저, 시종 씨에게서 벗어나고, 집에서 도망치고 싶었다. 그뿐이었다. 그냥, 싫어진 것을 참고 싶지 않았다. 도망친다고 하더라도 그녀는 딱히 갈 곳이 없었다. 물론 돈도 한 푼 없었다. 시종 씨는 쯔이에게 일절 돈을 주지 않았다. 그도 쯔이를 완벽하게 믿지 못했다. 쯔이가 한국에 와서 알게 된 사람이라곤, 남편과 관련된 사람들밖에 없었다. 그녀는 다문화가정 모임에도 나가지 못했고, 말이 통하는 같은 나라에서 온 친구도 주변에 없었다.

실제로 남편은 쯔이가 가진 전부였다. 그녀는 그에게서 도망치겠다고 결심했을 때에야 그 사실을 깨달았다. 그렇지만 적절한 기회와 시간이 오게 되면 결코 찾을

upset.

Shi-jong decided that he would get his younger brother married this year, no matter what. The very next day, he would go right to the bank and get information on the loan. How terrible he felt about his brother, working the farm for his older brother and growing old, never having his own life. What pity he took on this younger brother, just eating his meals, his head down, and the older brother shed tears, without any explanation.

The husband continually told his young bride that everything was going to be okay. It was strange, but whenever she heard him say those words, she felt as though everything were about to go wrong. So it was that at these moments when he was there with her, she would be miserable. And it seemed that worse might be ahead, to be brought on by the way she felt. Some time ago, Thuy had gone to a gynecologist in town and had an abortion, a secret kept from Shi-jong, and it seemed to her that this had been the origin of ill fortune, which frightened her. She had now been in Korea for five months, and it had gotten so that her eyes would just stare out on empty space. Time flowed slowly for Thuy, ever and slowly on.

수 없는 곳으로 도망갈 생각이었다. 그럼에도 그런 생각의 끝은 여전히 막막하기만 했다. 그래도 어딘가는 있을 것만 같았고, 누군가를 다시 만날 것만 같았다. 새롭게 시작할 수 있을 것만 같았다. 그것은 불행하기만 한 일은 아니었다. 다시, 한국에서 인생을 새롭게 시작할 수 있을지도 모른다고, 그런 생각의 끝에는 왠지 자신이 곧 행복해질 것 같은 희망이 생겨났다.

쯔이는 오솔길을 따라 마을 뒷산에 올라가곤 했다. 한 시간쯤 작은 산길을 따라가다 보면, 큰 나무들이 여러 그루 모여 있는 평평한 곳이 나왔다. 뒷산에서 자라는 나무들은 키도 작고 볼품없는 것들이 대부분이었는데, 그곳의 나무들은 크기부터 분위기가 달랐다. 나무 한 그루의 넓이가 어른 서넛이 팔을 벌려 안아도 그 품이 넉넉히 남을 만큼 거대했다. 쯔이는 거대한 나무에 기대고 앉아서 노래를 불렀다. 〈아름다운 대나무〉라는 노래를 좋아했다. 사랑을 잃고 떠도는 아름다운 처녀를 대나무에 비유한 노래였는데, 자신의 처지가 그런 것 같아 구슬펐다. 고향의 대나무 사이를 오가는 바람 소리가 그리워졌다.

She came to spend more time just sitting, her mind devoid of thoughts. She did not take up any of the work assigned to her each day, and the accumulation of tasks was like a mountain. It was only natural that her mother-in-law was hard on her, and increasingly so. She hated everything, and there was nothing that did not bother her. Married life in Korea, it seemed to her, had been a failure, even before it had begun. And the worst of it was having no affection for her husband, this old man on whom she had to rely and with whom she had to live.

"Husband. Hey. There's...a smell...strange...from your body."

"What, what're you talking about? And to me, just washed."

Shi-jong went over himself with his nose, sniffing. From then on, Thuy would hold her breath as well as she could manage, whenever her husband approached. There was about him a repulsive smell that was difficult for her to bear. She couldn't be sure if the odor was real, and maybe it wasn't. Because of the odor, though, it was hard for her to be anywhere near her husband. Every time they had intercourse, she had to hold her breath, almost

한번은 남편이 그곳으로 쯔이를 찾아 올라온 적이 있었다. 올해로 53세인 시종 씨는 땀을 삘삘 흘리면서 처음으로 무서운 표정을 지었다.

쁘이, 일하다 말고 사라지면 어쩌자는 것이여?

화가 났다기보다는 이곳까지 쯔이를 찾으러 온 것이 짜증이 난 모양이었다.

이곳에 오면 안 뒤야. 여긴 성황당이라 무당들이나 오는 곳이여. 무당 알아? 무당 말이여. 요렇고롬 생긴 것 걸치고 춤추믄서, 하는 무당 말이여.

시종 씨가 무당들이 추는 춤을 흉내 냈다.

쁘이, 아냐. 뿌이, 아냐. ……쯔이, 오케이? 내 이름 쯔이.

쯔이는 자기의 이름을 또박또박 말해주었다.

그러니깐, 쁘이. 하여간 여기 오면 안 된다고. 여기, 귀신 살아. 귀신 알아? 요롱게롬 생겨갖고……

내 이름, 쯔이. 쯔이입니다!

토라진 쯔이가 성큼성큼 앞서 산을 내려갔다.

뿌이, 아니, 쁘이, 거 서봐. 왜 성을 내고 그려.

그가 뒤에서 불렀지만, 쯔이는 못 들은 체했다.

to the point of killing herself. It was fortunate that her husband would go out to sleep in his aged mother's room after intercourse.

"Oh, I love my little Poo-wie."

Thuy got goose-bumps over her arms every time he said this. Her husband was sometimes moved to pity her, and it was at such times that he would tell Thuy that he loved her. This occurred only once in a while, but he did on occasion feel sorry for his young bride, who had come here from a distant land to enter the house-hold of a husband. When he thought of how hard their life was, there in the country-side, he felt even worse. Still, this consid-eration was not anything that might have inspired gratitude; it only made Thuy uncomfortable. There was nothing about him that she could like. From the first, that was how it had been.

Thuy wanted only to get away from him, and to escape from this house. That was all. She would not abide what was to her so vile. Even if she were to escape, though, there would be no place for her to go. Of course, she did not even have any mon-ey. Shi-jong never gave her money. He couldn't quite bring himself to trust Thuy. And the only people with whom she had had any contact since

쯔이는 제법 한국말을 잘했다. 말을 잘 알아듣고, 한글도 제법 쓰고 읽을 줄 알았다. 그런데 막상 한국에 와서는 한국말을 쓰기가 싫어졌다. 그냥, 알아듣지 못하고, 말하지 못하는 척하는 게 쯔이는 편했다. 그녀는 하노이에 있는 외국어학교에서 한국어를 2년 동안이나 공부했다. 일반적인 고등학교 말고 전문적인 외국어학교에 진학해서 쯔이는 한국어와 영어를 전공했다.

쯔이는 고등학교를 졸업하자마자 한국으로 시집을 오게 되었다. 한국에 가게 되었다는 사실만으로도 반은 성공한 것처럼 보였다. 모든 것이 기대했던 것과는 정반대였지만.

쯔이는 누군가 훔쳐보는 것을 진즉에 알고 있었다. 욕실에 나 있는 조그만 창은 누군가 일부러 부순 것처럼 보였다. 아니, 그렇지 않을 수도 있지만 쯔이는 누군가 일부러 그래 놓은 것이라고 확신했다. 욕실의 작은 창문은 창틀의 홈이 뒤틀려 언젠가부터 닫히지 않았다. 창문은 화장실에 나 있는 것치고는 꽤 커서, 보려고 마음만 먹으면 멀리서도 안이 훤히 들여다보였다.

화장실 창문, 안 닫혀. 시종 씨가 고쳐줘.

coming to Korea were those connected to her husband. She could not attend the "multi-cultural" meetings organized for international residents of the area, and she had around her no friends, no one who had come from her country, no one with whom she could have a conversation.

In fact, all Thuy had was her husband. This occurred to her when she decided to run away from him. Yet she made up her mind, and if the chance were to come and at the right time, she would run away, to some place where she could not be found. However, the conclusion of such thoughts was still vague. And yet it seemed to her possible, that she could be somewhere else, and that she could again meet someone. She could make a new start. Ill fortune was not all there was. Perhaps she could start a new life, here in Korea, and at the end of this thought, somehow, there was a hope of being happy again, and soon.

Thuy used to go along the path that ran behind the village and up the mountain. After an hour's walk, the narrow mountain path emerged onto a piece of level ground where there were several towering trees. The impression made by even just the height of these trees was in distinct contrast

나이도 애린 년이, 남편에게 시종 씨가 뭐여. 시방님,
여보님, 요롱코롬 불러야지.

　시어머니가 옆으로 누운 채로 그녀를 나무랐다.

　이 산골에서 누가 본다고 그랴. 죄다 노인네들밖에 없
구만. 걱정 말어, 쁘이. 나중 시간 나면 고쳐놀 팅게.

　노모 옆에 누워 있던 남편이 무심하게 말했다.

　가족들은 그냥 저렇게 시간을 좀 보내면 좋아지겠지
했다. 농사의 일손이라야 이제껏 해오던 것이었으니,
특별히 더 일손이 필요한 것도 아니어서 시종 씨는 쯔
이가 하고 싶은 대로 그냥 내버려두었다.

　무신, 돈 처발러서 들인 며느리라는 것이 할 줄 아는
게 암껏도 없음시. 밥만 늘었네, 허이고, 참.

　노모의 타박에 남편은 머리만 긁적였다. 남편은 쯔이
가 점점 나아지고 있다고 생각했다. 쯔이의 표정은 더
욱 심드렁해지고 우울해졌지만 그는 알지 못했다. 시골
생활에 적응하지 못하고 답답해하는 쯔이를 위해 매일
전주로 놀러 나갈 수도 없는 노릇이었다. 전주에 가봐
도 뾰족한 수가 없었다. 쯔이는 오래되고 점잖은 도시
의 풍경이 흥미롭지 않았다. 트럭을 몰고 나가 외식도

with that of the trees growing in the hills behind the house, most of which were small and rather meager. They were also of gigantic circumference, so that if three or four adults joined hands and tried to stretch their arms around one, some distance might be left. Thuy would sit down against one of these enormous trees, and she would sing. There was a song that she liked, called "Beautiful Bamboo." The song made a comparison between a beautiful girl who wandered about, having lost her love, and a bamboo, and she thought of how sad her own situation was, like that of the song. How she missed the sound of the wind, passing through the bamboo of her home-town.

Thuy's husband once went there, looking for her. Shi-jong, who was fifty-three that year, was sweating very hard and for the first time, he looked very angry.

"How come you disappeared in the middle a' work like that, Puy?"

Rather than angry, now it seemed that he was annoyed at having had to come such a distance in search of her.

"An' you ain't s'pose t'be here. This is a shrine, to the god a' this place, so it's for shamans, and like

하고, 향수를 달래기 위해 베트남 쌀국수도 먹어봤지만, 그때 잠시뿐이었다. 더군다나 남편은 점점 쯔이와 함께 외출하는 것을 꺼렸다. 사람들의 곱지 않은 시선 때문이었다.

그래도 봄 햇살은 가끔 매혹적이었다. 겨울이 끝나가던 무렵, 쯔이가 맛보았던 한국의 추위에 비하면 가히 아름다운 날씨임이 분명했다. 쯔이가 처음 한국에 왔던 3월, 봄이 시작되는 날씨였음에도 쯔이는 꼭 얼어 죽을 것만 같았다.

지렇게 오돌오돌 떰시롱, 겨울은 어떻게 함시롱 견딜까잉.

시어머니가 이불을 뒤집어쓰고 TV만 보고 있는 어린 며느리를 쳐다보며 푸념을 늘어놓았다. 완전한 봄이 되자 쯔이는 조금 달라졌다. 밤에는 제법 쌀쌀했지만 낮에는 춥지도 덥지도 않았다. 고향의 겨울과 제법 기후가 비슷해지는 시기였다. 쯔이의 마음도 날씨 탓에 조금은 누그러졌다.

지천에 핀 벚꽃이 쯔이의 마음을 다스려주었다. 다음은 라일락, 그리고 아카시아까지 연이어 터지는 꽃 잔

that. You know what shamans is? Shamans. Clothes all colorful, and dancin' around, like this, shamans, you know?"

Shi-jong imitated the dancing of a shaman.

"Not 'Puy'. Not 'Poo-wie'...'Thuy', okay? My name. It's 'Thuy'." Thuy spoke her name clearly for him.

"Sure, okay, Puy. Anyway, y'ain't s'pose t'be here. There's ghosts livin' here. Ghosts, you know? Look like this..."

"My name. 'Thuy.' My name is *Thuy!*"

Now sullen, Thuy stomped off down the mountain path ahead of him.

"Poo-wie. Puy, no! You stop, right there. What're you angry for?"

He called out from behind her, but Thuy pretended she hadn't heard him.

Thuy did know the Korean language, and she was quite good at it. She could understand it well, and she could also read and write very well in the Korean script. Yet she preferred not to use Korean, she once had actually come to Korea. Pretending she that could not understand or speak just made things easier for her. She had studied Korean for two years at a foreign language academy in Hanoi. This was instead of a regular high school, a pro-

치에 어린 이국의 신부 마음도 조금 누그러지는 것 같았다. 아카시아 향기가 바람을 타고 깊숙한 산골 마을에 떠다녔다.

어둠 속에서 지켜보던 눈길을 알아챈 건 쯔이가 아카시아 향기에 흠뻑 취해 있을 무렵이었다. 그 향기는 기분을 좋게 만드는 마력이 있음이 분명했다. 소리를 지르지도 않았고 겁이 나지도 않았다. 처음부터 자신의 알몸을 훔쳐보는 사람이 누구인지 그녀는 알고 있었다. 어쩌면 창틀이 휘어져서 창문이 닫히지 않았던 때부터 누가 이런 짓을 했는지 쯔이는 짐작하고 있었다. 여자의 본능이고 직감이었다.

쯔이는 모른 척, 샤워를 할 때면 그쪽에서 자신의 알몸이 더욱 잘 보이도록 창문에 정면으로 섰다. 쯔이의 작지만 굴곡 있는 몸이 주위 어둠 속에서 적나라하게 드러났다.

아카시아 아래 웅크리고 앉은 어둠 속의 눈을 그녀는 똑바로 바라보았다. 그녀는 오래도록 욕실 창가에 서 있었다. 비누칠을 하며 자신의 몸을 어루만지기도 하고, 자신의 은밀한 부분을 의도적으로 만지기도 했다.

fessional school of foreign languages, where her majors had been Korean and English.

Right after her graduation from high school, she had come to Korea, to join the house-hold of the husband. Being able to leave and actually go to Korea, it seemed to her that one half of her goal had been achieved, even if everything was exactly the opposite of what she had expected.

Thuy knew that someone was watching her. The small window in the bathroom was broken, apparently on purpose. It was possible that this was not the case, but Thuy was sure that someone had done this, and that it had been deliberate. Because the frame of the small window in the bathroom was bent out of shape, it had not been possible for some time to draw the sash at all. Through the window, the interior of the bathroom would have been visible to anyone who wished to look, even from a distance.

"The bathroom window... It's not closing... Shi-jong, you fix it."

"You, callin' yer husband 'Shi-jong', at yer age?" scolded her mother-in-law, lying there on her side. "'Husband' you call him, or 'Dear'."

Her husband, seated next to his old mother, said

47

모든 행동은 아카시아 아래 어둠 속을 향해 있었다. 시간이 흐르면서 쯔이는 뭔가 확신을 할 수 있게 되었다. 아카시아 뒤에 숨어 자신의 몸을 훔쳐보는 그가 이곳을 벗어날 수 있게 해줄 거라는 희망이 그것이었다. 생각이 거기에 이르자 쯔이의 몸짓은 더욱 적극적으로 변해 갔다.

기종 씨가 어린 형수의 알몸을 처음 본 것은 순전히 우연이었다. 상황이 이 지경까지 이른 것에 그는 죽고 싶은 심정이었다. 이런 결말을 가져올 것이라는 것을 전혀 상상도 하지 못했었다. 쯔이도 조금은 의도적이었음을 그는 전혀 알지 못했다. 모두 자기의 잘못으로 생긴 일이라고 생각했다.

설거지도 미룬 채, 저녁 밥상을 옆으로 물러놓고 가족들 모두 꾸벅꾸벅 졸고 있었다. 켜놓은 TV에선 오래전 방영됐던 드라마가 방영되고 있었다. 노모는 코까지 골며 다디단 초저녁잠에 빠져 있었고, 형도 졸다 깨다를 반복하고 있었다. 기종 씨도 하릴없이 무슨 내용인지도 모르는 저녁 드라마를 건성으로 보고 있었다. 아주 일상적인 저녁의 풍경이었다. 오줌을 누려고 화장실에 갔

without concern, "Who'd be lookin', out here in the mountains? No-one but old folks, out here. Don't worry, Puy. I get some time later, I'll fix it."

The family thought she would improve with the passage of time. In the past, without her, the work of the farm had always been completed and had not required additional hands, so Shi-jong left her to do as she pleased.

"What? Put up that kind a' money to bring in this daughter-in-law, an' then she don't know how t'do nuthin'. We goin' through more rice, though. Shoot."

In response to these complaints from his aged mother, the husband would only scratch his head. The husband supposed that Thuy was getting better. He never noticed the expression of apathy and depression in her features, but it was growing. He couldn't be going all the way to Jeon-ju every day just for Thuy's sake, just because she couldn't get used to life in the country-side and felt frustrated. And even when they did go to Jeon-ju, they had few options. Thuy had no interest in the sights of the city, old and respectable though it was. Driving there in the truck, they would go out to eat, and they would have Vietnamese rice noodles as a

던 기종 씨는 안에서 샤워를 하고 있는 소리를 듣고 밖으로 나갔다.

기종 씨는 그 처음을 생각하면 절대로 의도적이 아니었음을, 스스로에게 변명하곤 했다. 때때론 그 순간이 억울하게 느껴지기도 했다. 집 뒤꼍에서 오줌을 누던 기종 씨는 우연히 화장실 창문 틈으로 샤워를 하고 있는 어린 형수의 몸을 보게 되었다. 한 뼘쯤 열려 있는 문틈 사이로 쯔이의 아름답고 매끈한 몸이 감칠맛 나게 엿보였다. 그의 발걸음이 자기도 모르게 그쪽으로 향했다. 그는 넋을 놓고 문틈에서 뿜어져 나오는 강렬한 빛앞에 서 있었다. 가무잡잡한 피부와 작은 몸, 잘록한 허리에서 엉덩이로 이어지는 아름다운 곡선, 몸에 비해 제법 큰 가슴에 그는 정신을 빼앗겼다. 군살이라곤 찾아볼 수 없는, 작지만 매끈한 몸매에 그는 혼을 빼앗겼다. 그 작은 문틈 사이로 쯔이의 모든 것을 보았다.

샤워가 끝나고 쯔이의 모습이 작은 틈에서 사라지자 그는 미쳐버릴 것만 같았다. 심장이 벌렁벌렁 요동쳤다. 곧 욕실의 불이 꺼지자 그는 심한 낭패감에 사로잡혔다. 그는 그 자리에 쭈그리고 앉아 조금 전 문틈으로

comfort for Thuy in her homesick condition, but the effects of this never went beyond the moment. And because of the disapproval in people's eyes, the husband was becoming more reluctant to being out with Thuy.

Still, the sun-light of the spring was at times enchanting. The weather was indeed beautiful, especially in comparison with the cold she had endured for a bit at the end of the Korean winter. Although she had first arrived in March, the month in which spring begins, she had felt as if she would freeze to death, then.

"Shaking like that, what she gon' do in winter?" The mother-in-law would grumble, looking at her daughter-in-law wrapped in a blanket and just watching TV.

When the spring had come and was in full bloom, a small change occurred in Thuy. Nights were still quite cool, but during the day it was neither too cold nor too hot. They were coming into a time that was similar to the winter of her own country. Because of the weather, Thuy's heart knew a measure of peace.

The cherry blossoms, in bloom everywhere, worked to soothe Thuy's heart. And then the heart

엿보았던 강렬한 환영을 되살려내려 애썼다.

오밤중에 어딜 갔다 오냐?

한참 만에 들어온 기종 씨에게 형이 무심히 말했다.

……이잉, 63번에서 송아지가 나올 때가 돼서, 전등 좀 켜주고 왔당게. ……오늘넬, 허잖여.

기종 씨는 아직도 채 흥분이 가라앉지 않은 걸 들킬 세라 얼른 망설이지 않고 둘러댔다. 형 시종 씨가 구성지게 방귀를 부웅, 뀌었다. 그의 외국인 형수는 방에서 음악을 듣고 있었다. 형이 사다준 조그만 시디플레이어에서 현란한 음악이 작게 새어나오고 있었다.

하따, 오늘은 졸립다잉. ……자야겠당.

그의 형이 늘어지게 하품을 하며 기종 씨의 눈치를 보았다. 말을 하고서도 한참 동안 TV에서 눈을 떼지 않은 채로 배를 긁었다.

기종 씨는 늙은 엄마 옆에 슬며시 누웠다. 고단한 늙은 엄마의 코 고는 소리가 적막한 밤을 더욱 쓸쓸하게 하는 것 같았다. 형이 슬쩍 일어나 기종 씨를 힐끔거리더니 방으로 들어갔다. 기종 씨는 눈을 감았다. 감은 눈 속에서 어린 형수의 몸이 어른거렸다. 곧 슬며시 방문

of this young bride, this foreigner, must have been soothed some by the lilacs and then the acacias, and by this festival of flowers in which all came into bloom, one after another. Carried along on the wind, the fragrance of the acacias flowed into the village, deep in the mountains.

It was in those days, while the fragrance of the acacia was so intoxicating, that Thuy became aware of a pair of eyes, out there in the dark and watching her. The power of the fragrance must have been like that of an enchantment, as under it she was set at ease. She didn't cry out, and she wasn't frightened. And from the time it began, she had known who it must be, stealing this view of her naked body. She had been able to guess who would commit such an act, even when the frame of the window had just gone warped and the sash first refused to close. She had instinct, and she had the intuition of a woman.

Whenever taking a shower then, she would stand facing the window, pretending to be oblivious, and from there she would offer a clear view of her naked body. Although Thuy was small, the curves of her body were visible and clear against the outer darkness.

이 열고 닫히는 소리가 들리고, 찰칵, 문을 잠그는 소리가 들려왔다. 방 안에서 현란한 아이돌 그룹의 노래가 밀려나왔다 사라졌다.

기종 씨는 눈을 껌벅이며 천장을 멍하니 바라보았다. 이제 팔순이 가까운 노모의 코 고는 소리가 귓가에 쩌렁쩌렁 울렸다. 기종 씨가 고개를 돌려 고단한 잠을 이어가고 있는 노모의 얼굴을 바라보았다.

방 안에서 어린 형수의 가느다란 신음 소리가 들려왔다. 그것은 꼭 환청 같아서 신경을 곤두세우며 들으려고 하면 어디론가 날아가버렸다. 그의 가슴이 다시 요동치기 시작했다. 가늘게 새어 나오는 이국인 형수의 신음 소리와, 늙은 엄마의 코 고는 소리와, 아이돌 그룹의 노랫소리와, 낮은 볼륨의 TV 소리가 외롭고 적막한 산골의 고요함을 더욱 침잠시켰다.

기종 씨가 늙은 엄마를 거칠게 흔들어 깨웠다.

엄니, 엄니. ……언능 들어가서 자. 감기 걸링당게.

기종 씨는 다음 날, 아예 문이 닫히지 않게 펜치로 화장실 창틀을 휘어놓았다.

She would look right out, straight towards the eyes lurking in the dark, out there below the acacia trees. And there she would be for quite a while, right in the bathroom window. As she spread the lather around, she would caress her body, and with deliberate care she would reach down and touch herself there. Every move was directed out into the dark, under the acacias. With the passing of time, a certainty grew within her. This was her hope, that the one who was hiding himself behind the acacia tree and stealing this view of her body would liberate her from this place. When her thoughts had come to this point, her actions took on a more energetic quality.

It was entirely by accident that Ghi-jong had first seen the naked body of his young sister-in-law. The situation having evolved to this point, he almost wanted to die. It had not been within him to imagine that any such results would occur. Nor had he ever known how Thuy's own intentions had been involved in this. He thought he alone was at fault for all of what happened.

Having set the table set aside, and putting the dishes off, the family were dozing. There was a soap opera on TV, an old one that had been shown

그녀가 감쪽같이 사라졌다. 베트남에서 한국으로 시집온 지 반년이 지나고 있었다. 남편은 어안이 벙벙했다. 집집마다 돌아다니며 수소문해보았지만, 그녀를 봤다는 사람은 없었다. 마을로 들어오는 버스 운전기사에게 물어보았다. 운전기사는 친절하게 무전으로 사정을 알아봐주었다. 무전으로 마을에서 버스를 탄 외국인이 아무도 없었다는 소식이 날아왔다. 시종 씨는 안절부절 못했다. 지난 여섯 달 동안, 들었던 정 때문에 마음이 미어지는 것 같았다. 그보다 그녀를 데려오는 데 값비싸게 치른 돈 때문에 그의 마음이 더욱 공허해졌다. 꼭 사기라도 당한 기분이었다. 아직 사실을 모르는 동생에게 무어라고 얘기해야 할지도 난감했다. 어렵게 마련한 결혼 생활이 이렇게 허무하게 마무리되리라곤 예상치 못했다. 시종은 꽁꽁 숨겨두었던 그녀의 여권을 꺼내보았다.

이거 없인, 암 데도 못 가는디, 도대체 어디로 간겨.

남편은 신부의 여권을 펼쳐 사진을 멍하니 바라보았다. 맥없이 눈물이 흘렀다. 그녀의 물건이라고 해봐야 별 게 없었으니, 사라진 물건이 도대체 무엇인지도 그

years earlier. The aged mother had dropped off into the sweet sleep of early evening and was snoring, while the older brother was nodding off, waking and nodding off. Ghi-jong gazed with an absent mind at the evening soap opera, not knowing what it was about. It was a typical evening scene. Ghi-jong had to relieve himself and was going out to the bathroom, but hearing the sound of the shower, he instead went on out to the back.

Ghi-jong would think back on how it had happened without any intention, that first time, trying to make excuses. Sometimes he even felt that the moment had been unjust. As he stood behind the house relieving himself, Ghi-jong had happened to catch sight of the open bathroom window, and of the body of his young sister-in-law, taking a shower. The window was open by a gap about as far across as the breadth of a hand, and there Thuy's beautiful body appeared, smooth and tempting. Without knowing it, he took a step in that direction. And then captivated, he had just stood there, with the window before him and a vibrant light radiating through the gap. Her dark skin, her diminutive stature, the beautiful curve that ran from around the slender waist up and over the hips, and her

는 알 수 없었다. 시종 씨의 늙은 엄마는 집 안에 없어진 물건이 없는지 확인하고는 머리를 싸매고 앓아누웠다. 그녀의 입에서 상스런 욕들이 쉴 새 없이 방언처럼 터져 나왔다. 늙은 남편은 도대체 그녀가 어떻게 어디로 간 것인지 궁금해서 죽을 지경이었다. 별의별 생각이 짧은 시간에 복잡하게 얽혔다. 혹시라도 뭐가 잘못된 것이 아닌지 걱정이 앞섰다. 심정은 더욱 암울해졌다.

형수님. ……이럼시롱 안 되는디, 시방 내가 뭔 짓을 하는 거시……

뒤따라온 기종 씨가 성황당에서 어린 형수를 후박나무 아래, 우악스럽게 눕혔다. 용기와 자제력의 상실이 순식간에 교차됐다. 그녀는 아무런 반항을 하지 않았다. 시동생과 형수의 밀회는 그렇게 시작되었다.

처음이 어려웠지, 두 번, 세 번, 이후는 대수로운 일이 아닌 게 되었다. 시간이 지날수록 시동생도 형수도 아무런 가책이 없어졌다.

쯔이는 낮에는 시동생을 상대하고, 밤에는 남편을 상대해야 했다. 작은 몸은 두 남자를 상대하기에 버거웠지만 악착같이 참아냈다. 아버지뻘 되는 두 남자를 상

breasts, which were quite large in proportion with the rest of her, all caused his senses to fail. He lost himself to this small, smooth body, on which the flesh was not one bit in excess. Through the small gap in the window, he gazed on Thuy, and he saw everything.

Afterwards, when the shower was over and the image of Thuy had disappeared from the small gap, he felt as though he would go mad. His heart, beating away, went wild. The bathroom light was turned off, and immediately he was seized by a severe sense of failure. Crouched there, he tried to call back to mind the intense vision he had just beheld through the gap in the window.

"Well, where you been, this time a' night?" said the older brother, though without any real concern, as Ghi-jong came back in after such a long absence.

"...Ah, it's about time for number sixty-three's calf, so I turned a light on for her... It don't come tonight, got t' be tomorrow, yeah?"

Determined to prevent the discovery of his excitement, from which he had not yet been able to calm himself, Ghi-jong was quick to come up with the story, and without hesitation. Older brother

대하는 것이 여간 곤혹스러운 일이 아니었다. 그녀는
꼭 참았다.

나, 임신했어. 시동생, 아기.

기종 씨는 이제껏 자신이 무슨 짓을 한 것인지 그 말
을 듣고서야 깨달았다. 쉰이 다 된 나이였지만 이러한
상황을 어떻게 해결해야 하는지 알지 못했다. 혹시라도
엄마와 형이 이 일을 알게 되기라도 할까 봐 전전긍긍
했다. 그가 더욱 두려웠던 것은 바로 형의 부인, 자기의
아이를 임신했다고 말하는 어린 외국인 형수였다.

나, 어쩍해. 시동생.

그녀가 또박또박 시동생을 발음할 때면 차라리 마을
둠벙에라도 빠져 죽고 싶었다.

나, 애기, 나? 형, 알면, 죽어. …… 엄마, 알면, 나,
죽어.

쯔이는 자기가 임신한 아이가 누구의 아이인지 알지
못했다. 어떻든 상관없었다. 어차피 낳아서는 안 될 아
이임이 분명했고, 이렇게 어린 나이에 아이를 낳아서
기르고 싶은 생각도 없었다. 어떻게든 이곳을 벗어나
도망치기 위한 방법이라고 그녀는 밀려드는 가책을 마

Shi-jong let out a sonorous fart. In her room, the foreign sister-in-law was listening to music. The muffled tones of some flashy song escaped from the small CD player that his older brother had bought for her.

"Shoot, I'm tired tonight. Goin' t' bed."

The older brother yawned, long, and then checked Ghi-jong's face. In spite of what he had said, he just scratched at his belly and went on gazing at the television screen for some time.

Ghi-jong lay down there, gently next to his aged mother. With the snoring of his tired old mother, there was an increase in the loneliness of this lonely night. Stealthily, watching Ghi-jong out of the corner of his eye, the older brother rose and moved off towards the bedroom. Ghi-jong closed his eyes. With his eyes closed, he was haunted by the body of his young sister-in-law. Presently there came the sound of the door as it was opened and then closed, and then he heard the click of the lock. From the bed-room, the flashy music of some young pop group was pushed out and then was gone.

Ghi-jong blinked his eyes and stared up at the ceiling. The sound of the snoring of his aged

음 가장자리로 밀어냈다.

기종 씨는 형수를 산부인과에 데리고 갔다. 이런저런 핑계를 둘러대느라 그는 애를 먹었다. 물론 엄마와 형은 아무런 낌새도 채지 못했다. 의심을 사지 않기 위해 산부인과에 다녀온 날에도 그녀는 남편을 받아들여야만 했다. 읍내에서 몇몇 사람이 알은체를 해서 기종 씨의 얼굴은 사색이 되었다. 좀더 먼 곳으로, 전주로 나갈 것을, 하고 그는 후회했다. 쯔이의 말만 믿었지, 그녀가 임신한 아이가 자기 아이가 아닐지도 모른다고 생각한 건 한참 후였다. 그렇든 그렇지 않든 상관없는 일이었다. 어차피 낳아서는 안 되는 아이라는 것만은 그도 분명히 알고 있었기 때문이었다.

어떻게 이렁 수가 있냐잉.

집으로 돌아온 동생을 붙잡고 형이 울면서 혀 꼬부라진 소리를 했다. 그는 얼마나 울었는지 눈두덩이 팅팅 부어 있었다.

······내가 욕심이 많아가지고잉, ······니 돈까장 다 써불고잉, ······니 장개도 못 보내주고잉······

시종 씨는 목이 메어 말을 잇지 못했다. 형의 말을 모

mother, who was now almost eighty years old, reverberated in his ears. Ghi-jong turned his head, and he looked at the face of the aged mother, who remained within her tired slumber.

From the bedroom, he seemed to hear a faint moan from his young sister-in-law. It was so exactly like an auditory hallucination, though, that when he listened for it then, and strained with every nerve, it seemed to have flown away. Again, his heart was wild, beating away. In that lonely and desolate stillness, the stillness itself deepened with that faint moan from his foreign sister-in-law, a slip of which seemed to have just escaped, and with the sound of his aged mother's snoring, the sound of that pop group, and the sound of the TV, turned down low.

Ghi-jong shook his mother hard and woke her up.

"Momma. Momma... Go on t' bed now, to your room. Go on, it's gettin' cold."

The next day, Ghi-jong bent the frame of the bathroom window with a pair of pincers, so that the sash could not be drawn at all.

She disappeared completely. A half year had passed since she had come from Vietnam to Korea,

른 척 들어야만 하는 동생의 마음도 함께 찢어지는 듯
했다. 기종 씨는 형의 넋두리를 아무 말 하지 않고 들어
주었다. 완전히 술에 취해 고꾸라진 형을 기종 씨는 업
어서 방에 뉘였다.

쯔이를 군산의 미군 클럽 근처에 데려다 준 것은 기
종 씨였다. 짓누르는 양심의 가책 때문에 그는 한집에
서 쯔이와, 형을 마주 보기가 힘들었다. 누군가는 집에
서 나가야 했지만, 갈 곳 없기로는 기종 씨도 쯔이와 마
찬가지였다. 도망치겠다고 제안한 그녀가 오히려 고맙
기까지 했다.

시동생, 도와줘, 아무 곳에나, 데려다 줘.

그, 시동생이라고 부르지 좀 말랑게. ……아주, 기냥
섬뜩햐.

잠시 고민할 틈도 없었다. 그는 군산 어딘가에 있다는
미군부대가 떠올랐다. 차라리 그 편이 서로들을 위해
낫겠다는 생각이 들었다. 결심하자 모든 것이 순조로워
졌다. 쯔이는 들뜬 표정을 지었다. 그는 조금도 망설이
지 않고 쯔이를 그곳에 데려다 주었다. 물론 아무도 눈
치를 챈 사람도, 그들을 본 마을 사람도 없었다. 쯔이는

to enter the house-hold of the husband. The husband was at a loss. He went around and checked at every house, but there was no-one who had seen her. He asked the driver of the bus that came to the village. The bus driver was sympathetic, and he got on the radio and asked around at the station. The report that flowed out from the radio, though, was that there had been no foreigners on any bus from the village. Shi-jong was growing anxious. Having had such affection for her for six months, it seemed that his heart was in agony. Or rather, his heart was being hollowed out, as it were, with the expensive loss of all the money he had spent to bring her. He felt like he had been swindled. He didn't know what he would say to his brother, who wasn't yet aware of the situation. It was certainly nothing he had ever expected, that the marriage should end in vain like this, after he had put so much into bringing it off. Shi-jong got out her passport, which he had hidden well, and looked at it.

"Can't go nowhere, without this. So where's she gone?"

The husband opened the bride's passport and just stared at the photo. Tears made their way

감쪽같이 사라져버린 게 되었다.

일주일도 못 돼서 그녀를 다시 데려와야겠다고 결심한 것은 형과 늙은 엄마 때문이었다. 생각했던 것보다 그들이 겪는 충격은 꽤 큰 듯했다. 도무지 마음을 잡지 못하고 형 시종 씨는 술만 먹었다. 먹었다 하면 전에 없었던 술주정을 부리며 울고불고 난리가 아니었다. 쯔이를 그리워하는 마음, 쌓였던 정 때문이 아니었다. 욕심 부려 과용해서 얻은 결혼이 실패로 끝나버린 것과, 또 동생에게 미안해서 그는 매일 술을 마셨다.

노모는 금쪽같은 큰아들이 그렇게 된 것이 마음 아파 견딜 수가 없었다. 노모의 입에서는 입에 담기조차 더러운 쌍욕들, 쯔이를 저주하는 말들이 쉴 새 없이 터져 나왔다. 형과 노모를 보며 기종 씨도 참혹한 마음을 감출 길이 없었다. 형에게 시집온 그녀가 원망스럽기까지 했다.

지난밤, 술에 취해 쓰러졌던 형이 잠에서 깨자마자 또다시 소주를 대접에 부어 마셨다. 그의 눈은 며칠 동안 이어진 폭음으로 빨갛게 충혈되어 있었다. 동생이 술을 따르던 형의 손을 붙잡았다.

down. There had been almost nothing that could have been considered her own, so there was no obvious absence of things to be seen. Shi-jong's aged mother went to bed, sick, once she had gone through the house to see if anything was missing. Crude profanity would explode from her mouth, as though she were speaking in tongues. As for the old husband, he strained himself almost to death with conjecture over how and where she could have gone. He had all kinds of thoughts, and these had become a tightly tangled mesh in no time. Thinking about what might have happened, he was worried. His mood became darker, and bleak.

"Sister-in-law... I shouldn't be doing this. What am I doing?..."

There at the shrine, having followed his young sister-in-law, Ghi-jong had brutally forced her down under the silver magnolia. Audacity had flashed within him, entwined with a loss of control. She gave no resistance. In this way had begun a secret affair between the brother- and sister-in-law.

It had been difficult, the first time, but as things progressed through the second, the third and so on, it became nothing serious. Time passed, and

성님, 미안혀어. ……내가 쥑일 놈이랑게.

동생 기종 씨는 형 시종 씨에게 형수와 있었던 일을 하나도 빠짐없이 얘기했다. 동생의 말을 가만히 듣고 있던 형의 손이 부들부들 떨렸다. 울먹이며 말하는 동생에게 형이 소주를 대접에 가득 부어주었다.

……일단, ……찾아오고 보자잉.

시종 씨의 입에서 차분하게 가라앉은 쇳소리가 흘러나왔다.

다행히 쓰이는 군산을 떠나지 않았다. 한 클럽에서 그녀를 찾아냈다. 다시 집으로 데려오는 일은 간단했다. 월세 방을 얻느라 빚진 돈만 물어주었다. 쓰이를 차에 태울 때까지 동생 기종 씨는 그녀의 허리춤을 움켜쥔 손을 한 번도 놓지 않았다.

저는, 행복하고, 싶어. 놓아줘. 부탁입니다.

지럴허네, 시벌년.

운전대를 잡은 시종 씨가 험악하게 쓰이를 째려보았다. 시종 씨와 기종 씨 형제 사이, 그녀는 아무 말도 하지 못하고 앉아 있었다. 만약, 둘 중 한 명이 나타났다면 어떻게든 설득하고 저항도 해보았을 테지만, 둘이 같이

the brother- and sister-in-law came to have no remorse.

So Thuy would have her brother-in-law to accommodate during the day, and then at night there was her husband. With two men, it was not easy for her small body, but she was determined to persevere, and she bore it. There was also the extreme humiliation of accommodating two men who were both as old as her father. And with intense struggle, this too, she bore.

"I am...pregnant. Brother-in-law, it's...a baby."

When he heard these words, Ghi-jong became conscious of what he had been doing up to that point. Though almost fifty years old, he didn't know how such a situation could be solved. He was worried, afraid that his mother and his older brother would find out about it. And what frightened him more was his older brother's wife, this young sister-in-law who had told him that she was pregnant with his child.

"What do I do? Brother-in-law."

At her clear pronunciation of "brother-in-law", he wished that he were in the village reservoir, drowned.

"Me? A baby...Me...? Your brother, if he knows, I

나타난 것이 예사롭지 않았다. 그것이 두려워서 쯔이는 얌전히 형제를 따라 그들의 집으로 돌아왔다.

지나놓고 보면 살면서 후회되지 않는 일이란 매 순간 거의 없는 것이겠지만, 쯔이는 그날, 형제들이 모는 트럭에 절대로 올라타서는 안 되었다. 그녀가 그들의 집으로 돌아왔을 때, 이제는 누구도 호의적인 사람이 없었다. 심지어 노모는 그녀를 보자마자 머리채를 휘어잡았다.

이런 도둑년, 오늘 내 손으로 작살을 낼 것이여.

노모의 부아가 얼마나 들끓었던지, 형제가 아무리 떼어놓으려 해도 그녀의 머리카락을 휘어 감은 손을 놓지 않았다.

쯔이를 찾으러 가는 트럭 안, 형제는 한참 동안 서로 아무 말이 없었다. 두 시간가량을 달려 군산 초입에 다다랐을 무렵, 형이 무겁게 입을 열었다.

······니 말을 듣고 봉게, 내가 너한티, 더 참, 미안터라고잉. ······원래는 화가 나고잉, 너를 때려 쥑여버려야는디잉, ······암시랑통 안 허드랑게.

······

will die... Mother, if she knows, I will die."

Thuy didn't know whose it was, the child with which she was pregnant. However, she didn't care. She was convinced it was a baby that should not be born, and she didn't want to raise a child at this young age. Telling herself it was all her way out of this place, she pushed aside the guilt that had come over her.

Ghi-jong took his sister-in-law to the gynecologist. He had a very hard time of it, making excuses. Of course, his mother and brother never even had a clue. And in order to prevent any suspicion, she had later had to accommodate her husband, even on the day she had been to the clinic. In town, some people had said hello, and Ghi-jong's face had gone very dark with shame. 'Should've gone farther, some other place, some place in Jeon-ju.' Regret. He was convinced, after what Thuy had told him. Not until much later did he give any thought to the idea that the baby might not have been his. But whether it was his or not made no difference. He was absolutely certain that this baby should not be born, in any case.

"How come this hadda happen?"

Crying, and with a twisted tongue, the older

그려서잉, 곰곰맨치로 생각 좀 해본게……, 내가 말여, 갸를 부인으로 생각한 게 아니드라고. 나이 차도 많이 나기도 허고. ……좀체 들어간 돈 생각만 나고, 그러드란 말이여잉. 좀체가 뿌이가 평생 베필이라든지, 아도 낳고, 그런 부인처럼 느껴지지가 않았던 말이여잉. 기냥, 돈 주고 사온 여자맨치롬 기냥 그렸단 말이여. 물론 잘도 해보려고 노력도 해봤쌌었는디. ……잘 안 되드라고잉. ……그려서 곰곰맨치로 더 생각 좀 해본게. ……너만 갠찮음, 같이 셋이 잘 살아봄시룽, 어떨까 하더란 말이여잉. 그려도, 난 갠찮을 것 같더라고.

운전을 하며 형의 말을 무거운 마음으로 듣고 있던 기종 씨의 눈이 휘둥그레졌다.

그렁게롬, 성님, 말씸이……

긍게, ……그려어, 거시기 하잔 말이여잉.

그들의 집으로 돌아온 후, 쯔이는 방 안에 갇혔다. 밖에서 자물쇠로 문을 잠그고 식구들은 일을 나갔다.

오메, 이젠, 내가 며누리 요강까지 비워주면서까정 살아야겄네잉.

시어머니가 요강을 방에 던져 넣으며 그녀를 타박

72

brother spoke to his younger brother, who had just come in. He had obviously wept a great deal, as the skin around his eyes had grown quite swollen.

"...So damn selfish, wa' n't I?... Even with the money pose ta been yers...an' I can't even get y' married..."

His throat seized up, and Shi-jong was able to say no more. Having to pretend not to know what his older brother was talking about, the younger brother felt as if his heart were being torn. Ghi-jong listened to his older brother's babble without a word. Then he took his thoroughly drunk and unconscious older brother on his back, carried him to the bedroom and laid him down.

It was Ghi-jong himself who had taken Thuy away and brought her there, to Gun-san, near a bar for U.S. soldiers. His conscience had not been able to bear the sight of both Thuy and his older brother in the same house. It had been imperative that someone leave, but there was no place for Ghi-jong to go, just as there was none for Thuy. And then when Thuy had suggested that she run away, he had felt rather grateful.

"Help me, brother-in-law. Anywhere. Please, take me away."

했다.

쓰이는 방 안에서 하루 종일 TV를 보거나 음악을 들었다. 예전만큼 아이돌 그룹의 노래가 좋지 않았다. 드라마에 완전히 흥미를 잃어버렸다.

쓰이는 며느리도, 부인도, 형수도, 아무것도 아니었다. 형제는 그녀를 공유했다. 노모도 그 사실을 알고 있었다. 나무라기는커녕, 여전히 우애 좋은 형제로 남은 것을 다행으로 여겼다.

형제는 번갈아가며 시도 때도 없이 그녀를 탐했다. 축사에서 키우는 젖소만큼의 사랑과 배려도 쓰이는 받지 못했다.

쓰이는 모든 것을 포기했다. 그녀의 코리안드림은 거기까지였다.

방의 자물쇠를 풀고 쓰이를 꺼내준 것은 낮에도 일을 시키기 위해서였다. 형제들은 노모의 일이 줄어들게 된 것이 기뻤다. 효도하는 기분이 들었다.

쓰이가 성황당 후박나무에 목을 맨 것은 방에서 풀려난 다음 날이었다. 그녀가 한국으로 시집온 지 반년이 지났다.

"Enough a' that 'brother-in-law'... Don't sound right."

There had been no time for consideration. The U.S. army base, somewhere in Gun-san, had come to mind. They would each be helping the other, he thought. And once he had made up his mind, everything had gone well. Thuy had appeared excited. He hadn't hesitated at all, but had brought her right there, to that place. No one had suspected anything, of course, and they had not been seen in the village. And so the simple fact was that Thuy had just vanished.

In even less than a single week with his older brother and his aged mother, he decided he would bring her back. He saw how the shock of it had been far worse for them than he had imagined. Older brother Shi-jong did nothing but drink, not knowing how to pull himself together. Drinking, he would break into an alcoholic depravity that was without precedent for him, crying and hollering and making a mess. It wasn't that he missed her, or because of any affection he had accumulated since their marriage. Rather, it was because this marriage, based on his avarice, had now in fact failed, and also because he was sorry for what he had done to

후박나무에 대롱대롱 매달려 죽어 있는 쯔이를 마을 사람이 발견했다. 형제는 그녀가 다시 도망을 친 줄 알고 군산으로 트럭을 몰고 가던 중이었다. 후박나무 밑 놓여 있는 시디플레이어에서는 신인 아이돌 그룹의 현란한 노래가 흘러나오고 있었다. 시디플레이어는 베트남에서 쯔이가 늙은 남편에게서 혼수로 받은 것이었다.

쯔이의 장례식은 간소하게 치러졌다.

아무리 연락혀도, 연락이 안 닿는당게요. 이사 가버린 모양이요잉.

시종 씨가 난감하다는 듯이 형사에게 푸념을 늘어놓았다.

쯔이는 장례 의식 없이 화장해서 성황당 근처에 뿌려졌다. 그녀의 죽음에 관한 토막 기사가 신문 한 구석을 장식했는데, 그녀의 이름이 쁘이로 잘못 나왔다.

쯔이의 유골을 뿌리고 산에서 내려오면서 형 시종 씨가 동생 기종 씨에게 말했다.

한 1년쯤 있다가 말이여잉. 이번엔 니가, 장개가라고 잉. 평생 이렇고롬 살 수는 없응게. ……내가 가본께 너는 활달해서 우주베키스탄 애들하고도 잘 어울릴 것 같

his younger brother, that he drank every day.

The aged mother could not abide what was becoming of her precious older son. From her mouth
poured out profanity with which she cursed Thuy
in words that were foul beyond description. Ghi-
jong, seeing his older brother and his mother thus,
could not conceal the misery in his own heart. He,
too, got to making accusations against her, for
coming to enter the house-hold of the husband,
his older brother.

On the night before, the older brother had col-
lapsed, drunk, and upon waking, he started again,
pouring *soju* into a big bowl, and then he was
starting to drink. He had been drinking hard for
days, and his eyes were blood-shot. The younger
brother caught the hand with which the older
brother was pouring out the liquor.

"Older brother, I'm sorry... It was me, and I de-
serve to die."

The younger brother, Ghi-jong, had resolved to
tell the older brother, Shi-jong, all of what had
happened with his sister-in-law. As the older
brother listened in silence to what his younger
brother said, his hands shook, hard. And then the
older brother poured *soju* into the large bowl for

어. 그쪽도 아주, 갠찮애. ……늘씬하고 아주 갠찮애.

기종 씨가 생각만 해도 벌써부터 좋아 죽겠다는 듯 형을 보며 헤벌쭉 웃었다.

「힌트는 도련님」, 문학과지성사, 2011

his younger brother, who had wept as he spoke.

"...First...we get her back."

This emerged from the mouth of Shi-jong in a metallic tone, calm and settled.

Fortunately, Thuy had not left Gun-san. It was at the bar, that they found her. With ease, they were able to get her back, so that they could bring her home. They had only to pay what money she had borrowed for the rent of a room. Right up until they had put Thuy into the car, the younger brother Ghi-jong never once eased the hold he had around her waist.

"I want to be happy. Let me go. Please."

"Got a problem there, slut?"

In the driver's seat, Shi-jong glared at Thuy. Thuy sat between Shi-jong and Ghi-jong and couldn't say anything. Had it been just one of them, she would have tried to protest or resist, but it seemed too much for her, with both of them coming together like this. It frightened her, and so she went along with the brothers, quietly back to the house.

It may be that not a single moment of our lives will fail, in time, to arouse regret, but Thuy should truly not have gotten into the truck driven by the brothers that day. Once they were back at the house, no one was on her side. And as soon as the aged mother saw her, she actually seized her by the hair.

"The day's come, you filthy little thief, now I'm a tear you apart!"

The brothers tried hard to pull her off, but they could not get her to release her grip on Thuy's hair, so furious was her rage.

Back in the truck, on their way to retrieve Thuy, the brothers had passed some time in silence. After two hours of driving, they were getting close to Gun-san, and the older brother began to speak in a firm voice.

"...Hearin' what you tol' me, I'm just more sorry, is all... Maybe I'm s'pose t' get angry, and try an' kill you or somethin', but...it don't affect me like that."

"..." Ghi-jong said nothing.

"Well I been thinkin' serious about it...an' I see I never did take her on as my wife. We was too different, terms a' age...an' I wa'n't concerned w' nuthin' but the money I spent, so that's how it was, an' I never did think a' her as a companion in life, or as the wife who'd bear my child. As the purchase of a woman, for money, an' that's all. 'Course, I been tryin' t' get along with her, but...didn't work out... So I give it some more thought... If you're okay with it, maybe we could just go on, y' know, the three of us. Seems to me like that'd be the thing."

Ghi-jong was driving, and he listened with a heavy heart to what his older brother said, and then all at once, his eyes grew large.

"Hang on, older brother. Y' mean...?"

"Well, yeah...you know. Like that, yeah."

When they got back to the house, Thuy was put in the bed-room and confined there. They locked the door of the room from the outside and then went out to work.

"What's this? So now I got t' be cleanin' out a chamber pot for her?" complained the mother-in-law, tossing a chamber pot into the room.

In the room, Thuy would spend the whole day watching TV or listening to music. She didn't care much for those young pop stars and their music any more. Her interest in soap operas was gone, as well.

Thuy was not a daughter-in-law, not a wife, not a sister-in-law or anything at all. The brothers shared her. The aged mother was aware of this. She said nothing, though, relieved to see them still on good terms, as brothers.

Taking turns, the brothers might turn their desire on her at any time. Thuy never received even the love or consideration given to the cows being raised out in the shed.

Finally, Thuy gave up on everything. The dreams she had had of Korea ended there.

When they did open the door, and Thuy was let out, it was only so they could also have Thuy do some work during the day. The brothers were happy then, as there would be less work for their aged mother. They felt themselves to be doing what was proper for sons.

It was on the day after they had let her out of the room that Thuy hanged herself from a tree at the shrine. She had been married for a half year.

Some people from the village found her dead, hanging from the tree. The brothers had suspected that she had run away to Gun-san, and they had set out for Gun-san in the truck. Under the tree, the flashy music of the young pop group flowed out from a CD player. She had received the CD player as a wedding gift from her aging husband, back in Vietnam.

The funeral was minimal.

To the officer of the police, Shi-jong said, "Tried

and tried to call 'em. No answer. Maybe they moved," complaining in a way that suggested he felt awkward.

Without a proper ceremony, the body was cremated, and the ashes scattered near the shrine. There was a report about her death in the newspaper, where her name was incorrectly given as Puy.

After they had scattered her ashes and come down from the mountain, older brother Shi-jong spoke to Ghi-jong, the younger brother.

"Year from now, y' know. An' this time, you gon' out there and gon' be married. Y' can't live like this forever... Tellin' you, speakin' from experience, out-going guy like you, even get on well with one a' them Uzbekistani girls. Good ones, them. Real nice... Slim, I mean, not bad at all."

Looking at his older brother, Ghi-jong broke into a great big grin at just the thought of it.

Translated by Chang Chung-hwa and Andrew James Keast

# 해설

## Afterword

# 목 없거나 몫 없거나

안서현 (문학평론가)

## 리얼 혹은 그로테스크

백가흠의 소설은 늘 치명적이다. 끊임없이 폭력과 고
통에 관해 쓰는 그의 집요한 작가의식 때문이다. 그의
소설은 거대한 악에 의한 폭력이 아니라 우리 주변에
만연한 일상적 폭력에 관해, 범연하고도 서늘한 목소리
로 이야기한다. 그러면서도 날것 그대로의 강력한 고통
을 통해, 처연하고도 참혹하게 그것을 그려낸다. 이 '범
연'과 '처연'의 역설적 공존 속에 그의 소설 미학이 자리
한다. 이렇게 해서 탄생한 '일상적이지만 강도 높은' 고
통의 음각화(陰刻畵)는 독자의 폭력과 고통에 대한 감수

## Without a Voice, Without a Place

**Ahn Seo-hyeon** (literary critic)

**Real or Grotesque**

Fatality runs through all of Paik Ga-huim's stories. His literary conscience is insistent, and for this reason he is always writing about violence and pain. While they are told in a voice that is plain and calm, his stories deal with violence, though often of an ordinary kind, prevalent all around us, as opposed to the violence of any enormous evil. Moreover, through candid occasions of severe pain, these stories depict violence in ways that allow us to feel its cruelty and move us to pity. The beauty of his stories lies in their combination of profound sor-

성을 예리하게 자극한다. 그 고통은 늘 독자의 역치 값을 넘는 것으로, 현실에 대한 그들의 마비된 통각을 일깨운다. 그의 소설을 탐독하는 것은 곧 현실을 앓는 일에 다름 아닌 것이다.

그러한 그의 소설 속 서사는 때로 잔혹하다 못해 그로테스크하다는 느낌을 준다. 그러나 분명 그것이 현실이라는 것이 우리를 더욱 충격에 빠뜨린다. 현실적이지만 차라리 비현실적으로 느껴지는 가혹한 고통, 그것이 백가흠 소설의 요체다.

그러고 보면 「쁘이거나 쯔이거나」는 가장 '백가흠다운', 백가흠 소설의 한 전형을 보여준다 할 만하다. 이 작품 속에 재현된 한국적 가족, 그 속의 한국적 남성상, 그리고 그들에 의해 만들어진 한국적 젠더 현실은 더없이 현실적이다. 그러나 그 안에서 '쯔이'가 견뎌야 하는 폭력과 고통은 너무나 끔찍한 것이기에 오히려 비현실적인 것으로 느껴진다. 「쁘이거나 쯔이거나」는 이렇게 백가흠 식 '그로테스크 리얼리즘'의 세계로 독자를 초대하고 있는 것이다.

row with a guality of familiarity. Composition, in this case, seems to have been accomplished through the engraving of "common but intense" pain, as these works of art offend the reader's sensitivity to violence and pain. The pain here is pressed upon the reader's mind at all times, and its constant presence arouses a sensitivity to pain long since paralyzed. One might thus compare reading his work to feeling sickened by reality itself.

The descriptions given in these stories strike us as grotesque, as well as cruel. We are shocked then, upon consideration of how real they truly are. The essence of Paik Ga-huim's stories is realistic pain, submitted to us as if it was fantastic.

If we look at his work in this way, "Puy, Thuy, Whatever" is a typical example, and an excellent representative of what Paik Ga-huim does. The Korean family of this story, and especially its two Korean male members, are indeed quite realistic, as are the sexual conditions they create. The violence and pain that Thuy must suffer, though, are so horrible that one feels they cannot be real at all. Thus does the author use this story to invite us into his unique world of "grotesque realism."

## 코리언 드림 혹은 코리언 나이트메어

 덧없는 꿈을 꾸는 자는 가련하다. 그러나 자신의 꿈이 덧없다는 것을 잘 알면서도 그 꿈이라도 계속해서 꿀 수밖에 없는 자는 더욱 가련하다. 거짓 꿈에서 위안을 구하는 자. 백가흠의 「쁘이거나 쯔이거나」의 '쯔이'가 바로 이러한 인물이다.

 이 소설의 첫 장면은 그녀의 꿈이 여지없이 허물어지는 장면에서부터 시작된다. 그녀는 한국의 "가요와 드라마"에서 "천상에 사는, 이상과 꿈속에 사는 사람들"의 이미지를 읽었다. 그리고 자신과 결혼하여 한국에 가면 '동방신기'도 만날 수 있다는 '시종'의 말만 믿고 그 꿈을 좇아 무모한 한국행을 택한 것이다. 그러나 바로 다음 순간(이 소설의 첫 장면)부터 '쯔이'는 "믿고 싶었던 무엇이 막 허물어"지는 것을 느낀다. 한마디로 "뭔가 잘못됐다는 것을" 깨닫게 되는 것이다. 그 순간부터는 '시종'이 "모든 게 잘될 거"라고 하는 말조차 "모든 것이 엉망이 되어버릴 것만 같"다는 말로 바뀌어 들려오기 시작한다. 꿈이 악몽이 되는 것, '코리언 드림'이 '코리언 나이트메어'로 바뀌는 것은 그렇게 잠깐이다.

## Korean Dream or Korean Nightmare

Dreaming is a sad experience when its objects are empty or false. Even sadder, though, is when one becomes aware of the vanity and yet still cannot give up the dream. Such a dreamer is Thuy, the protagonist of "Puy, Thuy, Whatever," who searches for happiness through vain dreams.

The story begins with a scene where one can see her dream is already falling apart, and ruthlessly so. From "Korean pop songs and... serial melodrama," Thuy conceives of an image of "people who dwelled in paradise, who lived in the ideal and in dreams." When Shi-jong tells her that she'll be able to meet "Dong Bang Shin Ki" if she marries him and returns with him to Korea, she believes him and makes the foolish decision of moving to Korea in pursuit of her dream. In the very next event, then, the story's opening scene, Thuy feels "the crashing collapse of what she had been determined to believe in." Her realization here may be seen as her first "sense of something wrong" with the situation in general. From that moment on, every time Shi-jong assures her that "everything was going to be okay," it seems to her as if "everything were about

하지만 그녀는 여전히 꿈꾸기를 멈추지 않는다. '쯔이'는 꽃들이 피어나는 봄 풍경에 금세 "마음도 조금 누그러지는 것"을 느낀다. 그리고 "다시, 한국에서 인생을 새롭게 시작할 수 있을지도 모른다"는 환상을 붙든다. 그러나 봄꽃처럼 막 피어나는 자신의 육체와, 또 그 아름다움에 마음이 끌리는 시동생 '기종'의 마음이 더 큰 불행의 시작임을 그녀는 알지 못한 것이다. 그녀는 '기종'이 "이곳을 벗어날 수 있게 해줄 거라는 희망"을 품고 그에게 매달린다. 그녀가 '기종'의 아이를 임신하고 나서 '시종'을 피해 한 미군 클럽으로 도망쳤다가 다시 의기투합한 형제들에 의해 집으로 붙잡혀와 갇혔을 때, 그제야 그녀는 더 이상 "아이돌 그룹의 노래가 좋지 않"고, "드라마에 완전히 흥미를 잃"어버리게 된다.

그럼에도 불구하고 소설은 마지막 장면에서까지 "후박나무 밑[1] 놓여 있는 시디플레이어에서 신인 아이돌 그룹의 현란한 노래가 흘러나오고 있"는 것을 놓치지 않는다. 그 '시디플레이어'에서 우리는 그녀의 마지막 꿈을 본다. 스러지고 난 꿈의 형해(形骸)에라도 다시 매달려보는 한 인간의 모습을 보는 것이다. 막 진 봄꽃처럼 가련한 이야기다.

to go wrong." As dreams may sometimes collapse into nightmares, little time is required for this Korean dream to become a Korean nightmare.

And yet she refuses to quit dreaming. Looking out over the vistas of spring, so full of flowers, and all in bloom, Thuy "must have been soothed some." Again, she takes up her fantasy, and she imagines that she might be able to start another new life in Korea. She is not aware of the further adversities before her, whose seeds reside within her own body, and in her brother-in-law Ghi-jong's attraction to her, all coming into bloom with the flowers. Hoping that Ghi-jong "would liberate her from this place," she attaches herself to him. Only much later, after she has endured a pregnancy with Ghi-jong's child, after running away from Shi-jong to a bar frequented by American soldiers, and after she is brought back home and imprisoned by the two brothers—only then Thuy "didn't care much for those young pop stars and their music any more," and her "interest in soap operas was gone, as well."

And yet even then, for her final scene, "Under the tree[1], the flashy music of the young pop group flowed out from a CD player." With that CD player, we see once again what was to be her last dream.

## 관계의 상대 혹은 교환의 대상

결국 이 소설은 '코리언 드림'의 희생양이 되어버린 '쯔이'의 모습을 통해 두 '코리언' 남성, 즉 '시종'과 '기종' 두 형제의 남성적 폭력과 착취를 문제 삼는 것처럼 보인다. 그러나 그들 역시 한편으로는 순박하고 무지하고 가난한 여느 '농촌 총각들'로 보인다. 그렇다면 어디에서부터 모든 것이 잘못된 것일까. 처음 '시종'이 "고비용 결혼 프로젝트"를 통해 그녀를 데려올 때부터, 여성을 교환과 거래의 대상으로 삼는 거대한 물신적 구조에 참여하면서부터 이 참극은 시작된다. 다시 말해 이 소설은 직접적 가해자인 남성 인물들만을 비판적 시선으로 바라보게 하는 것이 아니라 더 큰 구조적 문제로 눈을 돌리게 하는 이중적 프레임을 갖고 있는 것이다.

내가 말여, 갸를 부인으로 생각한 게 아니드라고. 나이 차도 많이 나기도 허고. ……좀체 들어간 돈 생각만 나고, 그러드란 말이여잉. 좀체가 뿌이가 평생 베필이라든지, 아도 낳고, 그런 부인처럼 느껴지지가 않았던 말이여잉. 기냥, 돈 주고 사온 여자맨치롬 기냥 그렸단

This is an image of a human being holding on to a broken dream, even to its final destruction. Like the flowers of spring, withered only just now, the story is one of sorrow.

## People in Commercial Relationships

In one sense, this story concerns itself with the problem of violence and exploitation committed by males, the two Korean brothers Shi-jong and Ghi-jong, playing the part of aggressors and Thuy being rendered a victim of her "dreams of Korea." At the same time, though, these two brothers also resemble any other pair of country bachelors, poor and innocent. What, then, is the real source of the problem? The tragedy begins with the "expensive marital program" that Shi-jong finds himself engaged in to procure Thuy, taking part in this enormous materialistic system that reduces women to the objects of commerce, or merchandise for sale. In other words, one can view this story in either of two distinct frames: one in which we see and criticize the two male characters as the culprits, and one that allows us to see the problems with the entire system.

말이여. 물론 잘도 해보려고 노력도 해봤쌓썼는디.
……잘 안 되드라고잉. (72면)


　'시종'은 '쯔이'를 하나의 '상품'으로 여겼다. 그에게 그
녀는 "돈 주고 사온 여자"였다. "나이 어린 신부가 먼 타
국에서 자신에게 시집온 것이 안쓰럽고 불쌍하"다는 '연
민'은 있었지만, 그에게 그녀는 끝내 동등한 관계의 '상
대'가 아니라 '대상'에 불과하였던 것이 문제이다. 교환
의 대상은 다시 쉽게 연민의 대상이 되고 다시 본전을
뽑자는 생각에 기반한 성적 착취의 대상이 된다. 어느
편이든 그녀는 '대상'의 자리에 놓일 뿐이다. 그리고 동
생이 쓸 돈까지 써서 장가를 들었다는 데서 오는 미안
함에 대한 보상으로 그가 동생과 그녀를 "공유"하는 대
목에 이르면, 그녀는 형제간의 마음의 빚의 '대리보상
물'로서 이차적인 교환의 대상으로 전락하는 것이다. 그
리하여 그녀는 점점 "축사에서 키우는 젖소만큼의 사랑
과 배려도" 받지 못하게 된다. 인간을 관계의 '상대'로 받
아들이지 못하고 교환의 '대상'으로 삼는 세계. 인간을
'동물화'하고 '사물화'하는 차가운 관계. 이것이야말로 가
족이라는 사생활의 영역까지 침투한, 성역 없이 전 세

"'I see I never did take her on as my wife. We was too different, terms a' age... an' I wa'n't concerned w' nuthin' but the money I spent, so that's how it was, an' I never did think a' her as a companion in life, or as the wife who'd bear my child. As the purchase of a woman, for money, an' that's all. 'Course, I been tryin' t' get along with her, but... didn't work out.'"(81)

Shi-jong treats Thuy as if she were a mere 'product' of some kind. To him, marriage to her was "'the purchase of a woman, for money, an' that's all.'" He feels sorry for "his young bride, who had come here from a distant land to enter the household of a husband," but he sees her only as an object, never as a partner with whom to share an equal relationship, and this is the problem. An object of commerce easily becomes an object of pity, and then, for the sake of maximal return on money invested, she becomes an object of sexual abuse. Whatever her situation, her position is that of an object. Again, she falls into the position of an object of commerce when, motivated by an obligation Shi-jong feels for spending a marriage fund that had been meant for his younger brother, Shi-

계를 지배하는 거대한 '아웃소싱 자본주의'의 씁쓸한 자화상이 아닐까.[2] 이러한 거대한 구조 안에서 '시종'과 '기종'은 어느새 끔찍한 폭력적 기작의 허수아비가 되어버린 것이다.

그러니까 이 소설이 겨냥하는 것은 그러한 '차가운 관계'를 강제하는, 남성들에게 왜곡된 꿈을 제공하고 여성들에게도 그 기만적 꿈을 좇아오도록 만드는 현실의 환등상이다. 돈만 있으면 아내를 '사올' 수 있다는 꿈, "쪼매만 참"으면 돈을 모아서 동생에게도 "늘씬하고 아주 갠찮"은 우즈베키스탄 여자를 만나볼 수 있게 해주겠다는 꿈, 그러한 '시종'의 꿈은, 한국에만 가면 화려한 삶이 펼쳐질 것이라고 착각하는 '쯔이'의 꿈만큼이나 거짓된 것이다. 그들은 그러한 꿈을 꾸게 하는 미망의 환등상 안에 갇혀 있기에, 잘못된 꿈인 것을 알면서도 그 꿈에서 끝내 깨어나지 못하기에, 그러한 꿈으로 자신의 인생을 뒤흔들고 있기에, 가해자이면서도 한편으로는 제각기 가련한 존재들이다.

jong allows his brother to "share" his wife. And so she "never received even the love or consideration given to the cows being raised out in the shed." In these bleak portraits, set within a world where the human individual can be treated not as a partner but as an object of commerce, where one human being can become an animal or object to another, might we not discern the vast and "outsourcing capitalism" that holds dominion over every corner of the entire world?[2] Yes, it is under this enormous system that Shi-jong and Ghi-jong very quickly become puppets in odious and violent processes.

Among the story's intentions is the depiction of the real conditions that compel such cold, commercial relationships as these, relationships where men provide distorted, illusory dreams and use them to draw women into submission. And then there are the dreams of Shi-jong, who imagines that a man can get himself a wife through monetary transactions and that if a brother will only "'hang on, jus' a little more,'" then these same means of commercial exchange will likewise provide that brother with a woman from Uzbekistan: "slender an' all that, real nice." These are just as false as Thuy's dreams that a wonderful life can be hers if

## 목이 없는 혹은 몫이 없는

　최근 한국에서 이주여성의 삶에 관한 담론은 그 어느 때보다도 풍성하였다. 그러나 그러한 담론에서도 또다시 소외되는 '그녀'가 있다. 이 소설의 다음과 같은 대목을 보자.

　쪼이가 한국에 와서 알게 된 사람이라곤, 남편과 관련된 사람들밖에 없었다. 그녀는 다문화가정 모임에도 나가지 못했고, 말이 통하는 같은 나라에서 온 친구도 주변에 없었다. (34면)

　'다문화가정'에 대한 온갖 담론은 무성하지만, 모두가 소리 높여 '그녀들'에 대해 말하고 있지만, 사실 그 이야기의 '그녀들' 속에는 어떤 '그녀'가 빠져 있을지 모른다. 이 소설 속의 '쪼이' 역시 남편에 종속되어 이미 '없는 존재'나 다름없기에, 어떠한 '그녀들'의 이야기 속에도 등장하지 못할 뿐만 아니라 그녀 스스로도 세상을 향해 어떠한 발화도 할 수 없는 '목소리 없는 존재'가 되고 있다.

she only she goes to Korea. Both deluded, then, the characters are bound within a projected fantasy, not able to wake up even if they know, as they must, how wrong their dreams are. Their lives are shattered by those dreams; both characters are miserable figures deserving, even as twin culprits, of our deepest pity.

### Without a Voice, Without a Place

Foreign women who come to Korea as brides have been given much attention in recent discussions. In these discussions, though, writers tend to brush certain women aside. Consider the lines below:

"And the only people with whom she had had any contact since coming to Korea were those connected to her husband. She could not attend the 'multi-cultural' meetings organized for international residents of the area, and she had around her no friends, no one who had come from her country, no one with whom she could have a conversation."(39~41)

그러한 그녀의 열악한 소통 상황은 말이 통하지 않아서가 아니다. 그녀는 하노이 외국어학교에서 한국어를 공부하고 왔음에도 불구하고, 그녀의 남편을 비롯한 가족들과 제대로 된 대화를 나누지 못한다. 심지어 그녀는 자신의 이름을 알리는 데조차 실패한다. "내 이름, 쯔이. 쯔이입니다!"라는 말은 공허하게 울릴 뿐이다. 누구도 그녀에게 귀를 기울이지 않기 때문이다. 결국 그녀는 끝까지 자신의 이름을 되찾지 못하고, 죽은 후의 부고 기사에조차 "쁘이"로 이름을 올리게 된다. 이 '쁘이'라는 이름은, 이주여성으로서 그녀가 겪어야 했던 자기정체성의 상실을 상징적으로 드러낸다. 그뿐만이 아니다. 사람들의 시선 때문에 '시종'은 "점점 쯔이와 함께 외출하는 것을 꺼"린다. '기종' 역시 그녀에게 "그, 시동생이라고 부르지 좀 말랑게. ……아주, 기냥 섬뜩햐."라고 말한다. 결국 그녀는 자신의 본래 이름으로 불릴 수도 없고, 자신이 남편이나 시동생을 당당하게 부를 수도 없는 상황에 처한다. 그녀는 '부인이거나, 형수이거나' 상관없는 존재가 되어 정당하게 호칭을 부르지도 어떠한 호칭으로 불리지도 못하는 성적 대상으로만 남게 되는 것이다.

Yes, there has been a great deal of talk about "multi-cultural families." Everyone speaks of these women in animated voices, but among the women discussed, some women may yet be absent. In this story, for example, because Thuy is owned by her husband, she is a woman who virtually does not exist, and having lost her own voice, she is a woman who can say nothing to the world and thus would not appear in any conversation about these women.

This failure of communication is not caused by mere linguistic barriers. The story notes that Thuy has even learned Korean in Hanoi, having attended a special high school where foreign languages were the focus, and still she cannot communicate with her husband and his family. Indeed, she is unable to even convey the correct pronunciation of her name: "'My name. "Thuy." My name is *Thuy!*'" Her words, of course, are in vain. No one will listen to her. She cannot have her real name restored, and even in the notice of her death, her name is given as "Puy," this boggled name ultimately symbolizing the loss of identity that these foreign brides must frequently suffer.

And this is not all. Because of the looks they re-

쯔이는 며느리도, 부인도, 형수도, 아무것도 아니었다. 형제는 그녀를 공유했다. (74면)

한마디로 '쯔이'는 한국 사회의 온갖 '타자'에 관한 담론 속에서도 한 번도 호명되지 못한 소외된 존재이다. 길을 잃은 그녀를 나무라며 "이곳에 오면 안 뒈야. 여긴 성황당이라 무당들이나 오는 곳이여. (중략) 여기, 귀신 살아. 귀신 알아?"(38면)라는 '시종'의 말이 그래서 더욱 의미심장하게 들린다. 그녀는 '귀신'과도 같은 존재가 아니었을까. 자신의 목(소리)를 잃은 존재. 자신의 정당한 자리와 '몫'을 가지지 못한 존재.[3] 하여 이 소설의 또 다른 제목은 '목 없거나, 몫 없거나'가 될 것이다.

## 이야기의 끝 혹은 시작

이 소설의 마지막은 거대한 도돌이표와 같이, 다시 또 다른 '결혼 프로젝트'를 꿈꾸는 두 형제의 모습을 보여주는 것으로 끝난다. 끝이면서 시작이다. 비극의 순환이다.

그러나 이 소설은 우리 사회에서 목소리를 잃은 자들,

ceive in public, Shi-jong "was becoming more reluctant to being out with Thuy." Likewise, Ghi-jong reproaches her, "'Enough a' that "brother-in-law" ...Don't sound right.'" She is never called by her real name and the situation forbids her to address either her husband or bother-in-law without shame. The figure she has become may be "a wife, a sister-in-law, whatever," and as she can neither call others by their proper names nor through her own name demand just recognition, she is left as a mere sex object: "Thuy was not a daughter-in-law, not a wife, not a sister-in-law or anything at all."(83)

In a word, Thuy's situation is one of isolation; she is a figure who is never given a single mention in all the discussions of the various others who have come to populate Korean society. This imparts significance to the words spoken by Shi-jong: "An' you ain't s'pose t'be here. This is a shrine, to the god a' this place, so it's for shamans, and like that. [...] There's ghosts livin' here. Ghosts, you know?'" (45) Shi-jong scolds her for having wandered off. Thuy herself has been forced to exist as a mere shadow of a person. A person who has lost her voice, she is allowed neither a proper position as a wife nor an acceptable place anywhere else, and so

몫을 잃은 자들의 설 자리를 묻는 한편, 그들을 이곳으로 끊임없이 불러오는 거짓된 꿈에 관해서, 얼마간의 비용만 들이면 결혼을 할 수 있다는 꿈이나 혹은 한국에 오면 드라마 속의 주인공이 될 수 있다는 꿈을 생산—유포하는 자본과 미디어의 판타스마고리아에 대해서도 묻고 있다. 그리고 이 고통스러운 질문을 통해 독자는 이 비극적 '코리언 나이트메어'에서 깨어날 수 있다. 우리가 처음부터 다시 만나기 위하여, 우리가 처음 만나는 이야기를 처음부터 다시 시작하기 위하여, 그 무수한 새로운 이야기들의 새 판을 벌이기 위하여, 낡은 판을 끝내는 '풀이'와 '액막음'으로서 이 소설은 쓰여진 것이 아닐까. 그렇기 때문에 이 소설은 또 다른 의미에서도 이야기의 끝이면서 시작인 것이다.

고통받고 착취당하는 (여성의) 육체의 형상화는, '고통의 감수성'의 작가 백가흠의 한 장기였다. 그러한 그의 글쓰기는 늘 정치적 의미화의 가능성을 놓치지 않고 있음에도 주목하여야 한다. 이 작품 「쓰이거나 쯔이거나」역시, 날선 펜으로 날카로운 고통을 음각함으로써, 그 반대편에는 몫 없는 자들, 권력과 자본에 의한 내부 식민지 상태 속에서도 다시 남성에 의해 이중식민화되는

another title for this story might have been: 'Without a Voice, Without a Place.'[3]

### The End of the Story, or its Beginning

The final lines of this story seem to announce a return to old actions: the two brothers once again begin to dream about their next "marital program." Although it is the end, it is also the beginning. The tragedy of this story is cyclical.

Also, this is a story that raises questions: about giving positions to these people without voices and without any place in this society; about false dreams, such as those which motivate this perpetual flow of immigration; about capitalism; about the media and its dangerous illusions, which produce and spread the dream of marriage for anyone through nothing more than a sum of money, dream of transforming oneself into a character from Korean soap opera by simply Coming to Korea. Through these painful questions, readers may be awakened from the tragic course of this "Korean nightmare." Perhaps that is why this work was written; perhaps it was meant to bring this story of atrocity to a conclusion, and to work against fur-

하위 주체 여성의 문제를 돌올하게 양각해내는 데 성공하고 있는 것이다. 고통은 늘, 구원을 향한다.

1) 이 후박나무 밑은 '쯔이'에게 고향을 연상시키는 안식의 장소인 동시에 '기종'과의 밀회가 이루어지는 고통의 장소이다. 또한 그녀가 삶을 지탱하기 위해 찾아들던 장소이자, 그녀가 자기 손으로 죽음을 맞는 장소이기도 하다. 이와 같이 생과 사의 넘나듦을 보여주는 이 성황당 후박나무 밑은 마치 장편소설 『향』(2013)에서의 신비로운 숲과도 같은 상징적 공간이라 할 수 있다.
2) '아웃소싱 자본주의'에 관해서는 앨리 러셀 혹실드의 『나를 빌려드립니다』(류현 역, 이매진, 2013)가 진단과 통찰을 제공하고 있다.
3) 자크 랑시에르는 정치적 약자를 뜻하는 '몫이 없는 자들'에 관해 이야기하면서, 그들을 공동체 안에서 발언할 수 있는 자격이 주어지지 않은 존재라고 규정하였다. '말하기'와 '공동체 내 존재'를 연결짓고 있다는 점에서, 이러한 개념적 설명은 중요한 통찰을 제기하고 있다.

ther occasions of this atrocity, that we might meet again at the start and set out again with a story of meeting for the first time, given another chance for another new story. In this way, then, the story itself is both an end and a beginning in another sense as well.

With "sensitivity to pain" running throughout his work, Paik Ga-heum is famous for depicting the bodies of women afflicted by various forms of pain and abuse. But his writing might be understood in a political way as well. In "Puy, Thuy, Whatever," the acute pain of the victim has been successfully engraved with a razor sharp pen, but the image printed from this plate is a clear presentation of people without any place, showing the problems of women already conquered from within. They are conquered through power and money, rendered abject objects who must suffer a second conquest as they are later invaded by men. As always, pain shows us the way to salvation .

1) The shrine under the silver magnolia tree is a place of comfort for Thuy, reminding her of her hometown, and at the same time a place of pain, the location of her encounters with Ghi-jong. It is also both a place of life that Thuy frequents in order to sustain herself, and the place where her life ends by suicide. Thus, this shrine under the

silver magnolia, where we can see both life and death, is a symbolic place much like the mysterious forest in Paik's novel, *Incense* (2013).

2) Diagnosis of and insight into "outsourcing capitalism" is provided in Arlie Russell Hochschild's *The Outsourced Self* (Imagine, 2013).

3) Jacques Ranciere discusses "people without place," or the politically weak, whom he defines as people denied the right of speech in their community. With its connection it draws between "speech" and "existing within a community," this conceptual explanation offers us yet more critical insights.

# 비평의 목소리

Critical Acclaim

사회와 문화에도 무의식이 있는 바, 작가 백가흠만큼
만 솔직해지면, 우리는 우리 사회가 사실은 프로이트가
정식화한 바로 그 남성 신경증 환자들의 유아적이고 젖
비린내 나는 판타지에 얼마나 깊게 침윤되어 있는지 도
처에서 확인 가능하다. 그렇다면 백가흠의 소설은 어떤
측면에서 엄마를 찾아 삼만 리 아니라 영원의 거리까지
라도 떠돌 것만 같은 남아들이 점령한 이 불쾌한 사회
의 심리적 기원에 관한 이야기가 아닌가. 그렇다면 암
묵적인 형태로건 드러난 형태로건 남성들에 의해 매일
매일 자행되는 폭력의 연원으로서의 남성 판타지를 가
장 남성적인 방식으로 폭로하고 내파(內波)하는 작가,

Like the human individual, society and culture can also pass through stages of unconsciousness, and if we can be as bold as the writer Paik Ga-huim, we may be able to see everywhere the extent to which our own world is at its depths permeated by fantasy—infantile and still reeking of breast milk—of the male neurotic, a notion first formulated by Freud. Paik Ga-huim's works of fiction are, among other things, stories detailing the psychological origins of this absurd society, a world dominated by boys who seem to wander not for 30,000 *li* but forever in search of their mothers. And Paik Ga-huim himself is an artist engaged in the truly mas-

그가 바로 백가흠이다.

김형중

우리가 타인의 비극과 맞닥뜨리는 것은 언제나 짧은 한순간이 아니던가. 인내를 모르는 우리는 긴 시간을 버티지 못하고, 누군가의 고통을 만지는 일은 늘 너무나도 두렵다. 차라리 그렇게 사는 사람들과 그들을 그렇게 만든 사회를 맹렬히 비난하고, 채 몇 분도 지나지 않아 지워버리고 마는 우리다. 그러므로 지금 무엇보다 중요한 것은 그런 자동화된 반응을 차단하면서 그 삶을 다른 누구가 아닌 우리 자신의 삶의 문제로 옮겨오는 것이다. 만약 이 소설집 곳곳에서 당신을 기다리는 질문들이 당신을 위력적으로 집어삼키고 있다면, 그것은 단지 이 소설들이 우리가 망각하고 있는 삶의 한 단면을 재연하고 있어서가 아니다. 백가흠은 그만의 방식으로 우리 삶의 심연을 고찰하는 동시에 그 삶의 윤리를 고집스럽게 추궁하고 있다.

차미령

이제까지 백가흠 소설을 두고 이야기되었던 많은 담

culine work of exposure and implosion, writing about those male fantasies that can be found behind violence in its various forms, some implicit, and some realized everyday.

Kim Hyeong-jung

Do we never encounter the tragedies of others for more than a passing moment? Still not familiar with patience, we are able to endure so little, and any contact with the pain of another is always a terrifying experience. We are harsh with our criticism of these criminals and of the society that produced them, and then after a moment we just erase these problems from our minds. It is of the utmost importance that we avoid the automatic reactions of that kind, and that we accept as our own those problems we tend to see in the lives of others. Yes, these stories may indeed present parts of our lives to which we are oblivious, but this is not the only way in which the questions waiting throughout the book shock and consume the reader. In his own way, and by his own methods, even as he contemplates the abyss within our lives, Paik Ga-huim is conducting an insistent interrogation of the moral dimensions of those lives.　　　　Cha Mi-ryeong

론들, 예컨대 '남성의 신경증적 판타지'(김형중, 「남자가 사랑에 빠졌을 때」, 『귀뚜라미가 온다』, 문학동네, 2005; 김영찬, 「비루한 동물극장」, 『비루한 동물극장』, 창비, 2006.)라거나 '사도마조히즘의 극장'(복도훈, 「축생, 시체, 자동인형」, 『문학동네』, 2006년 여름호.)이라는 규정, 혹은 '비윤리적인 너무나 비윤리적인 포르노 르포르타주'(조연정, 「'충분히 근본적인' 교란을 위하여」, 『문학동네』, 2007년 봄호.)라거나 '축군의 그로테스크'(황종연, 「매 맞는 아이들의 정치적 상상력—2000년대 소설의 한 단면」, 『문학동네』, 2007년 가을호.) '현대의 비극'(차미령, 「바깥의 시선에서 안의 감각으로」, 『조대리의 트렁크』, 창비, 2007.)이라고 지칭하는 방식 등은 그 공감의 차이에도 불구하고 이 끔찍한 성적 혼란을 일종의 '지옥'으로 규정하고 있는 측면이 있다. 그럴 것이다. 어느 누구도 이 총체적인 삶의 뒤엉킴을 '신세계'의 도래라고는 받아들일 수 없을 것이다. 그것은 다만 인간 무의식 깊은 곳에 잠재된 동물적 본능과의 조우이자 우리 문명이 감추고 있는 괴물 같은 야만과의 대면일 수도 있다. 그러나 돌이켜보면 이 혼란은, 비록 '웰컴'을 외치며 환영할 만한 것이라고 할 수 없을지는 몰라도, 오늘 우리가 당연하게 생각하는 지배적인 성정체성을 교란시키고 의아하

Even if marked by some degree of sympathy, the discussions we've seen of Paik Ga-huim's work tend to find therein a horrific, sexual chaos which they regard as a "hell" of some kind, often referring to his stories as "neurotic male phantasies,"(Kim Hyeong-jung, "When a Man Falls in Love," published with *The Crickets Are Coming*, MunhakDongnae, 2005); (Kim Young-chan, "Poor Animal Theatre," from *Poor Animal Theatre*, Chang-bi, 2006) "sado-masochistic theatre,"(Bok Do-hun, "Animal, Corpse, Automaton," in *MunhakDongnae—Summer*, 2006) "highly immoral pornographic reporting," (Jo Yeon-jeong, "For the Thoroughly Fundamental Disturbance," in *MunhakDongnae—Spring*, 2007) "the axis of grotesquerie,"(Hwang Jong-yeon, "The Political Imagination of Abused Children—One Dimension of the Stories of the 2000s," in *MunhakDongnae—Fall*, 2007) and as some form of "modern tragedy"(Cha Mi-ryeong, "Looking From the Outside to the Sensitivity of the Interior," with *Mr. Jo's Trunk*, Chang-bi, 2007). Well, of course they are. No one could accept such total distortions of life as a "new world." Yet these stories are nothing else but encounters with the bestial instincts that reside deep inside the human consciousness, and within the monstrous barbarism hidden within our culture. Looking on this confusion, no, we do not accept it

게 만드는 계기를 함축하고 있다. 과연 오늘 우리가 정상으로 간주하는 성적 관습과 사유의 방식은 어디에서 왔는가? 혹 그것은 우리 문명이 상상해낸 하나의 허구는 아닐까. 그 질문 속으로 기꺼이 월경해 들어가는 것은 그리 끔찍하기만 한 경험은 아닐 것이다. 백가흠의 소설들이 우리에게 전해주는 전율은 이 물음으로의 아슬아슬하지만 흥미진진한 초대에 가깝기 때문이다.

신수정

「쁘이거나 쯔이거나」는 백가흠의 이전 소설이 보여주었던 여성에 대한 공격적 폭력성이 상대적으로 남아 있는 거의 유일한 소설이라고 할 수 있다. 하지만 이 소설에서 농촌에 시집 온 베트남 신부를 성적 착취의 대상으로 삼는 쉰이 넘은 농촌 총각과 그의 동생은, 어떤 폭력적인 남성성의 존재이기보다는 상대적으로 성의 교환과 분배에서 차별받는 사회적 주변부의 하위 주체들이다. 오히려 이것은 하나의 하위 주체가 전 지구적으로 또 다른 하위 주체를 착취하는 구조를 적나라하게 드러내준다. 코리안 드림을 가진 어린 신부 '쯔이'가 한국에 와서 당하는 성적인 착취에 대해 이 소설은 다만

with any ease, but this implicates the problematic dominant sexual identities we consider normal and provide an opportunity for us to challenge them. What are the origins of these sexual customs and these ideas regarding sex that we assume to be normal today? Are these not civilization's fictional inventions? Taking up such questions is far more than nasty experience. Through such questions, Paik Ga-huim's stories stimulate us, so that while his work is indeed dangerous, it is also like an exciting invitation.

Shin Su-jeong

The story "Puy, Thuy, Whatever" does include the violence against women that Paik Ga-huim presented in his earlier works. In addition to being the violent male figures of this story, though, the provincial old bachelor and the younger brother who sexually abuse the former's Vietnamese wife can also be seen as subordinate subjects on the margins of society, victims of discrimination in the exchanges and relative distribution of sex. Here we are given a frank exposition of an exploitive system, a world in which one subordinate subject will take advantage of another. While the story provides

냉정하게 묘사하고 있으며, 형인 시종 씨가 성교에 집착하는 이유는 다만 '쯔이'에게 들인 돈 때문이다. 자신의 이름 '쯔이'를 제대로 발음조차 하지 않고 '쁘이'라고 부르는 남편이라는 존재와 자신을 훔쳐보았던 그의 동생은 크게 차이가 나지 않는다. 형제를 동시에 상대할 수밖에 없는 끔찍한 착취의 상황은 그들, 소외된 농촌 남성들이 처한 성적인 소외를 충격적으로 보여준다. 결국 성황당 후박나무에 목을 맨 뒤에도 형제는 우즈베키스탄으로 새로운 성적 대상을 찾아가려 한다. 한국 안에서 성적인 교환의 상대를 찾을 수 없는 그들은 이미 거세된 하위 주체들이라고 할 수 있다.

이광호

a cold description of the sexual abuse suffered by Thuy, the young bride coming to Korea with a "Korean dream," it also explains how the monetary expense of procuring this wife was among the causes of the husband's obsessive need for sexual intercourse with her. This husband is not even able to pronounce "Thuy" and must instead call her "Puy," and his younger brother is not much different. The situation is repulsive, as Thuy must submit to and accommodate both of the brothers, but it shocks us also with its presentation of the extreme sexual marginalization of men in the country-side. In the end, the bride hangs herself from a tree in the forest primeval and the brothers react to this with plans to travel to Uzbekistan for their next sexual object. It could be said that these men, not able to find anyone inside of Korea to serve as objects of sexual exchange, are subordinate subjects, themselves, already castrated before the act.

Lee Kwang-ho

# 백가흠

　소설가 백가흠은 1974년 전라북도 익산에서 태어났다. 2001년 서울신문 신춘문예에 단편「광어」가 당선되면서 작품 활동을 시작하였다. 소설집으로『귀뚜라미가 온다』(2005),『조대리의 트렁크』(2007),『힌트는 도련님』(2011)이 있다. 초판 출간 당시 표지 색깔 때문에 '노란책'이라는 별명으로 불리기도 했던『귀뚜라미가 온다』는 인간 내면의 숨겨진 잔혹성을 고발하는 충격적 서사로 문단에 새로운 바람을 불러일으켰고,『조대리의 트렁크』에서도 역시 왜곡된 사회의 도덕성을 집요하게 문제 삼고 있는 수록작들을 통해 독자들의 '고통의 감수성'을 자극하였다. 세 번째 소설집인『힌트는 도련님』에서는 '소설쓰기'에 대한 성찰과 탐문을 담아내면서 작가의식의 새로운 전회를 보여주었다. 또 죽음을 앞둔 이들이 모여 사는 '하늘수련원'을 배경으로 생과 사가 공존하는 인간사의 비극적 본질을 그린『나프탈렌』(2012)과, 사후에도 계속되는 끈질긴 고통과 이를 통한 속죄와 구원의 문제를 탐구하고 있는『향』(2013) 등 묵직한

# Paik Ga-huim

Paik Ga-huim was born in the city of Iksan of Jeollabuk-do in 1974. In 2001 he made his literary debut, winning that year's *Seoul Shinmun* Spring Literary Contest with his story, "Halibut." In the subsequent years, Paik has produced three other collections of short stories: *The Crickets are Coming* (2005), *Mr. Jo's Trunk* (2007) and *The Hint is the Young Master* (2011). Often known as "that yellow book" in reference to the design of the first edition's jacket, *The Crickets are Coming* swept through the literary world as a new wind, shocking many with its vivid descriptions of the brutality of the human mind. The 'sensitivity to pain' of Paik's readers was stimulated by the stories in *Mr. Jo's Trunk*, as well, as these likewise discuss moral problems and the problems presented by a distorted society. In his third collection, *The Hint is the Young Master*, Paik puts the mental operations of a revolutionary writer on display, sharing his thoughts and raising questions about "the composition of fiction." His novel, *Naphthalene* (2012), depicts human history as essen-

장편소설을 연이어 출간하면서 독자적인 작품세계를 구축해가고 있다.

tially tragic, with life and death having a shared existence for the residents of the 'Haneul Center' waiting for death together. The next year saw the publication of a second novel, *Incense*, in which Paik conceives a pernicious agony that continues into the after-life and allows the author to address problems of atonement and salvation. The style Paik employs in his literary composition is his own, distinct and now well established.

**번역 장정화, 앤드류 제임스 키스트** Translated by Chang Chung-hwa (Chloe Keast) and Andrew James Keast

장정화는 2007년부터 한국의 현대 소설과 동화를 영어로 번역하는 일을 해왔다. 박성원의 소설 「캠핑카를 타고 울란바토르까지」를 공역하여 코리아타임즈 제44회 현대문학번역 장려상을 수상하였다. 박성원의 「도시는 무엇으로 이루어지는가」라는 단편소설집과 동화책 두 권은 한국문학번역원의 번역지원금을 받아 번역하였다. 2013년에 앤드류 제임스 키스트와 배수아의 「회색 時」를 공역하였고, 바이링 궐 에디션 한국 대표 소설 시리즈에 수록되었다.

Chang Chung-hwa has been working on the translation of Korean literature since 2007, with a focus on modern fiction and children's stories. She received the Modern Korean Literature Translation Commendation Prize sponsored by *The Korea Times* in 2013 with Park Seong-won's "By Motor-Home to Ulan Bator." For three of her projects—the collection of short stories, *What Is It That Makes Up a city?* by Park Seong-won, and two books for young children—she has been supported by grants from the Literature Translation Institute of Korea. In 2013, Ms. Chang collaborated with Andrew Keast on an English translation of Bae Su-ah's "Time In Gray," which was published in this series of Bi-lingual Edition Modern Korean Fiction.

앤드류 제임스 키스트는 박성원의 소설 「캠핑카를 타고 울란바토르까지」를 공역하여 제44회 현대문학번역 장려상을 수상하였다. 장정화와 공역한 배수아의 「회색 時」는 그의 첫 작품으로 2013년에 출간되었다. 한국문학번역원에서 박성원의 단편집 「도시는 무엇으로 이루어지는가」와 동화책 두 권으로 한국문학번역원에서 번역 지원을 받았다. 이외에도 여러 작품의 번역에 참여했으며 앞으로도 더 많은 작품의 번역, 출판에 참여하면서 언어적 기술을 더 연마하고자 매진하고 있다.

Working with Chang Chung hwa, Andrew James Keast received the Modern Korean Literature Translation Commendation Prize in 2013 for an English translation of Park Seong-won's "By Motor-Home to Ulan Bator." His first published work, a translation of Bae Su-ah's "Time In Gray," also produced in collaboration with Chang Chung hwa, was released in 2013. Mr. Keast has also worked on a variety of other projects, and three of these have been supported by grants from the Literature Translation Institute of Korea—two books for children, and Park Seong-won's collection of short stories, *What Is It That Makes Up a City?* He looks forward to the completion of more work for publication—and always to the further cultivation of his linguistic skills.

감수 **전승희, 데이비드 윌리엄 홍**

Edited by Jeon Seung-hee and David William Hong

전승희는 서울대학교와 하버드대학교에서 영문학과 비교문학으로 박사 학위를 받았으며, 현재 하버드대학교 한국학 연구소의 연구원으로 재직하며 아시아 문예 계간지 《ASIA》 편집위원으로 활동 중이다. 현대 한국문학 및 세계문학을 다룬 논문을 다수 발표했으며, 바흐친의 『장편소설과 민중언어』, 제인 오스틴의 『오만과 편견』 등을 공역했다. 1988년 한국여성연구소의 창립과 《여성과 사회》의 창간에 참여했고, 2002년부터 보스턴 지역 피학대 여성을 위한 단체인 '트랜지션하우스' 운영에 참여해 왔다. 2006년 하버드대학교 한국학 연구소에서 '한국 현대사와 기억'을 주제로 한 워크숍을 주관했다.

Jeon Seung-hee is a member of the Editorial Board of *ASIA*, and a Fellow at the Korea Institute, Harvard University. She received a Ph.D. in English Literature from Seoul National University and a Ph.D. in Comparative Literature from Harvard University. She has presented and published numerous papers on modern Korean and world literature. She is also a co-translator of Mikhail Bakhtin's *Novel and the People's Culture* and Jane Austen's *Pride and Prejudice*. She is a founding member of the Korean Women's Studies Institute and of the biannual Women's Studies' journal *Women and Society* (1988), and she has been working at 'Transition House,' the first and oldest shelter for battered women in New England. She organized a workshop entitled "The Politics of Memory in Modern Korea" at the Korea Institute, Harvard University, in 2006. She also served as an advising committee member for the Asia-Africa Literature Festival in 2007 and for the POSCO Asian Literature Forum in 2008.


데이비드 윌리엄 홍은 미국 일리노이주 시카고에서 태어났다. 일리노이대학교에서 영문학을, 뉴욕대학교에서 영어교육을 공부했다. 지난 2년간 서울에 거주하면서 처음으로 한국인과 아시아계 미국인 문학에 깊이 몰두할 기회를 가졌다. 현재 뉴욕에서 거주하며 강의와 저술 활동을 한다.

David William Hong was born in 1986 in Chicago, Illinois. He studied English Literature at the University of Illinois and English Education at New York University. For the past two years, he lived in Seoul, South Korea, where he was able to immerse himself in Korean and Asian-American literature for the first time. Currently, he lives in New York City, teaching and writing.

바이링궐 에디션 한국 대표 소설 065
쁘이거나 쯔이거나

2014년 6월 6일 초판 1쇄 인쇄 | 2014년 6월 13일 초판 1쇄 발행

지은이 백가흠 | 옮긴이 장정화, 앤드류 제임스 키스트 | 펴낸이 김재범
감수 전승희, 데이비드 윌리엄 홍 | 기획 정은경, 전성태, 이경재
편집 정수인, 이은혜 | 관리 박신영 | 디자인 이춘희
펴낸곳 (주)아시아 | 출판등록 2006년 1월 27일 제406-2006-000004호
주소 서울특별시 동작구 서달로 161-1(흑석동 100-16)
전화 02.821.5055 | 팩스 02.821.5057 | 홈페이지 www.bookasia.org
ISBN 979-11-5662-018-1 (set) | 979-11-5662-029-7 (04810)
값은 뒤표지에 있습니다.


Bi-lingual Edition Modern Korean Literature 065
Puy, Thuy, Whatever

Written by Paik Ga-huim | Translated by Chang Chung-hwa and Andrew James Keast
Published by Asia Publishers | 161-1, Seodal-ro, Dongjak-gu, Seoul, Korea
Homepage Address www.bookasia.org | Tel. (822).821.5055 | Fax. (822).821.5057
First published in Korea by Asia Publishers 2014
ISBN 979-11-5662-018-1 (set) | 979-11-5662-029-7 (04810)

## 바이링궐 에디션 한국 대표 소설 set 4

### 디아스포라 Diaspora

### 가족 Family

### 유머 Humor